ALSO BY ISABELL

The Ladies of Bath

The Duke's Daughter ~ Lady Amelia Atherton

The Baron in Bath ~ Miss Julia Bellevue

The Deceptive Earl ~ Lady Charity Abernathy

The Hawthorne Sisters

The Forbidden Valentine ~ Lady Eleanor

The Baggington Sisters

The Countess and the Baron ~ Prudence

Almost Promised ~ Temperance

The Healing Heart ~ Mercy

The Lady to Match a Rogue ~ Faith

Nettlefold Chronicles

Not Quite a Lady; Not Quite a Knight

Stitched in Love

Other Novels by Isabella Thorne

The Mad Heiress and the Duke ~ Miss Georgette Quinby

The Duke's Wicked Wager ~ Lady Evelyn Evering

Short Stories by Isabella Thorne

Love Springs Anew

The Mad Heiress' Cousin and the Hunt

Mischief, Mayhem and Murder: A Marquess of Evermont

Mistletoe and Masquerade ~ 2-in-1 Short Story Collection

Colonial Cressida and the Secret Duke ~ A Short Story

CONTENTS

THE DUKE'S WICKED WAGER

PART I
PROMISE ME A HANDFUL OF HORSES

Chapter 1	5
Chapter 2	13
Chapter 3	21
Chapter 4	31
Chapter 5	43
Chapter 6	51

PART II
PROMISE ME DARING

Chapter 7	59
Chapter 8	67
Chapter 9	75
Chapter 10	85
Chapter 11	95

PART III
PROMISE ME THIS DANCE

Chapter 12	109
Chapter 13	123
Chapter 14	133
Chapter 15	143
Chapter 16	153

PART IV
PROMISE ME YOUR HEART

Chapter 17	161
Chapter 18	167
Chapter 19	183

Chapter 20	195
Chapter 21	201
Sneak Peek of The Duke's Daughter	205
Chapter 1	207
Sign up for my VIP Reader List!	215

The Duke's Wicked Wager

Lady Evelyn Evering

Isabella Thorne

A Regency Romance Novel

The Duke's Wicked Wager ~ Lady Evelyn Evering
A Regency Romance Novel

All rights reserved.

This is a work of fiction. Names, characters, places and incidents are the products of the author's imagination and are used fictitiously. Any resemblance to actual persons, living or dead, events, or locales is entirely coincidental.

The Duke's Wicked Wager Copyright © 2016 by Isabella Thorne
Cover Art by Mary Lepiane

2016 Mikita Associates Publishing

Published in the United States of America.

www.isabellathorne.com

Part 1

Promise Me a Handful of Horses

1

*L*ady Evelyn Evering did not mean to eavesdrop... well maybe she did. It was hard not to. The door was cracked open and the voices inside were too loud to ignore. One of the voices belonged to her brother, Frederic. If he had a quieter way of speaking, she would have never heard the conversation. In the hallway, she crept closer and pressed her ear against the doorframe, holding the somewhat frayed ruffled hem of her mauve dress back so it would not be seen.

"She will not like this plan, Evermont." That was the Duke of Pemberton, George Pender. George was her brother's friend, acquired during their mutual pursuit of mischief.

"And yet, she will have no choice in the matter," Evelyn's brother, The Marquess of Evermont, said. "It is her duty to marry, and she will do it."

"Have you no kindness for your sister? She is an odd one, true, but does not seem to be a shrew. It would not be a bother to find her a husband she could grow to love. She does have a certain…grit."

There was a long pause, filled only by the just-audible inhales and exhales of cigar smoke. She could smell the earthy plumes of it wafting into the hall.

"It is marriage in a hurry or ruin for our family name" Frederic said at last.

"And this has naught to do with your latest flame, dear Adele? That pretty little actress is costing you a fortune to keep." The Duke replied.

Frederic snorted a laugh. The clink of crystal was followed by the sound of liquid pouring, and Evelyn could imagine the amber drink flowing from the decanter into their glasses.

"But Adele is worth every penny, my dear friend, for when I have done something to please her she will do her damnedest to please me." Frederic's smug smile was evident from his tone. "Isn't that the entire purpose of the gentler sex?"

Evelyn's cheeks burned at the rude talk and she spun away from the door. Servants edged out of her way, pressing back against the wallpaper to let her pass in a flurry of lace and ruffles. The house was not as staffed as it had been only a year ago, when her father still lived. They had been forced to let go some of the maids and footmen, but they managed. It was quieter without them, and without her father's booming laughter.

Her lip trembled as she stepped out of the house and made her way to the stable. It was some distance from the house, an immense, quadrangular structure that had at its prime housed sixty horses. Only a handful remained, but they were the twenty finest horses Evermont had ever boasted. Still, it was a sad state of affairs, and the beautiful white-stone complex seemed wasted for want of activity.

One of the grooms worked Valiant in the corral, putting the blood-bay through his paces. The stud was retired from his racing days but his elegant body still rippled with muscle beneath the dappled coat, and he sired the finest foals in all of Norfolk. She paused a moment to watch the stallion kick up the sand beneath his hooves. His steel shoes caught the sunlight. Her father had purchased Valiant when she was only a child but she could still remember the day the stallion had come home, all fire, calming only under her father's touch. He had been a master horseman, and a wonderful father. She missed him so. She brushed back the tears, determined not to cry again.

"A fine day for a ride, my Lady," said the stable master, Stanton, coming up beside her where she stood at the rail. "Shall I have Bellona saddled for you?"

Evelyn was tempted by the offer, smiling at the thought of the beautiful gray filly, but she was not dressed in her riding habit and that would require going back into the house with her brother.

"No, thank you, Stanton."

He reminded Evelyn of her father, though whether it was the similarity in their appearance or only that the two men had spent most of their days together and thus adopted similar mannerisms, she could not be certain. Regardless, his presence soothed her as her father's had.

"An inspection of the mares in foal, then?" he asked,

gesturing toward the barn. At her nod, Stanton led the way out of the dusty yard and into the coolness of the stone building.

The empty stalls dampened her spirits. They were swept clean, but Evelyn could picture every horse that should be there—horses that were already sold although their presence still filled her heart. Not ghosts, quite, but something like them filled the space now, as her father's memory did the house, a presence felt, but never seen. She could close her eyes and picture them, so many born right here at Evermont.

Modeste, a chestnut mare with an obscenely bulging belly, nickered at their approach. She was a placid, sweet-tempered thing, even in foal. Evelyn offered her palm to the mare and she pressed her white blazed nose there, snuffling for treats. Evelyn smiled at the feel of her velvet nose on her hand.

"Expectin' the birth this week now," Stanton said, reaching up to scratch the mare's neck. "An old pro, she is, should be no trouble at all."

"Let us hope for a colt. We cannot expect Valiant to live forever, though if any horse shall manage, it will be him." Evelyn patted Modeste in farewell and checked in on the other two pregnant mares.

They were not so far along as Modeste, but in the next few months they would have three new additions to the barn, if all went well. Two would need to be sold just after weaning, and potential buyers had already made offers. It pained Evelyn to part with any of Valiant's get. His line belonged at Evermont, but those were the ways of the past. She fingered the amethyst bracelet at her wrist, nodding as she half-listened to Stanton as he talked about the mares. A mark of her mourning, the bracelet felt as heavy as the burden of grief.

She had lost not only her father, but her betrothed as well. It had been a dark year at Evermont. Her fiancé had been killed in battle, a noble death for an officer, but one that had left her in shock. Their love had been a quiet one, of friendship rather than passion. He was eight years her senior, but he had been a kind, gentle man and she held him still in the greatest affection. Evelyn's father had made the match, selecting for her a husband with a love for horses and an open mind, a man who would not try to temper Evelyn's spirited ways. She had lost them both within a month of each other. What else could fate throw at her?

"My Lady?" Stanton was eyeing Evelyn with concern.

"Your pardon, Stanton, my mind was elsewhere. May I see the ledgers?" She had already looked at them ad nauseam. They did not change. There was nowhere else to save a farthing. If only her brother was not so loose with his cash.

The stable master's office was tidy and austere. A simple desk stood in the middle of the room and a window looked out over the pasture, where a few horses were grazing on the yellowed grass. Stanton offered her a chair, and pulled a thick stack of papers from a drawer in his desk. Despite its innocuous look, the ledger was an evil thing, listing out the shortcomings of Evermont's accounts in neat black figures. Evelyn schooled her features into a neutral expression as she went over the numbers with Stanton, but her emotions were a storm just beneath the placid surface.

Her brother sat somewhere in the manor, wasting his time discussing frivolous affairs over expensive brandy and expensive cigars, while the horses were meted out rations like soldiers on a long march. He planned to have her betrothed, only so his insatiable lust for tawdry women would not need to be tempered by restraint. Her blood boiled at the thought. At the bottom of it all was the Duke of Pemberton, a rake if she had ever known one. The ruin of Evermont lay at his feet, dragging her brother after him with his expensive ways.

"I cannot see any way around it. We shall have to sell another coach. Let the coachman select one, he will know best which one will fetch the highest sum. If it happens to be Frederic's favorite, well, that would be a shame." Her mouth was in a tight line.

"Of course, my Lady" Stanton said. "I will see to it this afternoon."

Evelyn closed the ledger book and pushed the chair back from the desk. She stood at the window and watched the horses for a moment, marveling at their grace as they took off in a sudden burst of speed, kicking up their hind legs and squealing.

"They are like children with their joy, are they not?"

"Very much so." Stanton had come to stand beside her, one age-spot speckled hand resting on the sill.

"And my foul brother will ruin it all for something as fleeting as smoke," Evelyn spat out. "He has no sense."

It was a bold statement to make to a servant, but

Stanton had become more than that to Evelyn since her father's death. Still, the stoic man took a moment to reply.

"If I may speak frankly, my Lady?" He waited for her nod before continuing. "I believe your father's passing affected you both in different manners. The Lord Evermont has found his own method of coping, as you have found yours."

He gestured to the barn surrounding them. It was true. She had always shared her father's interest in horses and had tagged along at his hip since she could walk, but it was not until he was gone that she had thrown herself into the world of it, taking charge as she had every right to.

"My grief does not tear the very house down around us." Evelyn squared her shoulders. "But I do not believe the blame is Frederic's alone, no, the Duke has been the impetus for it all. He has dragged my brother down to the depths of depravity, and only one of them has the means of crawling back out. He just does not see what he is doing to my brother—to us."

"Perhaps that is true, my Lady." If Stanton agreed with her, it was only his expression that told her so, for the man would not speak ill of one of the Peerage, despite his familiarity with Evelyn. "You are the only good thing your brother has, and it must be a heavy burden to bear."

"He does not treat me as if I am anything of worth. Just today he spoke of marrying me off!"

"Surely not, with you still in mourning?"

Evelyn threw her hands in the air. "My point, Stanton. He has lost all sense of propriety."

"If there is anything I may do for you, my Lady, you

only need ask," Stanton said. "I do not know what aid I may be, but—"

She shook her head. She had already asked too much of him, saddling him with her emotions as if he did not have matters to attend to, as short-staffed as she had left him. She lifted her head a bit, gaining control of her broiling emotions.

"Thank you, Stanton, but you have already eased some of my worries just by listening." Evelyn smiled at him, hoping it hid the tremor in her cheeks as she fought to keep the tears from betraying her. "I will leave you now, as I am sure you have a busy day ahead of you."

He bowed as she swept by him, and she wished for just a moment that he was her father, and he could wrap her in a hug so tight there was no room for her misery. But he was not, and she was alone on the walk back to the house, where nothing waited her but a fight with her brother. She could not avoid it for a moment longer. She cursed the impediment of her skirts as she made her way up the stairs, where the footman opened the door for her. If she were a man she would have engaged in fisticuffs with him to settle the matter, but she was not. She was a woman and she had little recourse. She hoped she could talk some sense into her obstinate brother.

"Where is Lord Evermont? I would speak with him with some urgency," she announced.

2

The butler, Mr. Pratt, appeared at Evelyn's side a moment later to escort her to Frederic. He was a discerning man; perhaps he had sensed the tension building in the air at Evermont and wished to keep the other servants from having a fight to gossip about. Her brother was alone in his study. The only sign of the Duke's presence was the empty glass and Frederic's apparent state of inebriation. It was probably best to wait to talk to him for he was belligerent when in his cups, but Evelyn could not put it off. Mr. Pratt left her at the doorway after she refused his offer for a tray of tea. She did not wish to give the appearance of this being a polite visit between siblings.

"Frederic."

He looked up from his book with red, unfocused eyes.

"Evelyn, my darling sister, have you come to scold me again?"

She put her hands on her hips, just beneath the stiff

boning of her stays. He was the older of them, but he had never acted it. In their youth, they had been close and had played together, but he had put Evelyn aside the moment he had turned old enough to shave. Though she had felt the loss keenly, she had found friends of her own and the distance between them had only grown into a comfortable sort of detachment. She had not thought of it before, but with her father dead, she was entirely dependent upon his whim. It was a frightening thought. Well, nonetheless, she was the stronger of the Evering siblings. She knew this, although she was younger by almost two years. She would manage this mess.

"Your odor offends, brother. Does your *actress* find the fetor of stale cigars appealing? But then, I imagine it smells as sweet as perfume, when compared to the stench of the hovel she lives in. She smells nothing but your money. How surprised she will be when she finds you have none."

Evelyn had not meant to begin with barbs, but it was too late to take them back. Her brother rose, face clouded with rage. He advanced on her and she could smell the brandy on him.

"Adele is twice the woman you could ever hope to be, Evelyn. She has poise, grace, and of course, beauty."

This was not quite fair. Evelyn had been complimented on her looks any number of times. If her black hair and pale complexion were not currently in vogue, well, they did not make her ugly.

"I do not care a whit about her, beyond the unseemly sum you have spent in the wooing of her."

"Our accounts are my affair. As my sister, you have no

part in them but for the dowry I choose to assign you. I choose!" he shouted.

He pressed her back until she hit the bookshelf.

"Evermont?"

The Duke of Pemberton stood in the doorway. Evelyn jumped. She had not seen him there, but now she did see him just over Frederic's shoulder, looking rumpled. He was always rumpled. His jaw was set in an angry line as he took in the scene. She used the moment of distraction to slip out beneath her brother's arm.

"Your Grace," Evelyn said, with a curtsy of respect. She really didn't like what her brother became around him, but he was a member of the Peerage. He deserved her respect, if not her affection.

"Lady Evelyn." The Duke inclined his head in gracious irony. "Lovely as ever, like a vision from beyond the grave."

Evelyn scowled. He had made pointed jokes about the paleness of her skin since the day they had met. The novelty had yet to wear off, it seemed.

"She was just about to leave," Frederic said.

"My brother is confused. I have only just arrived." Evelyn took the leather armchair in the corner for herself, sinking into it before her legs could succumb to the adrenaline that coursed in them from her brother's behavior. If the Duke had not entered, at the moment he did would Frederic have struck her?

She met Frederic's glare. Their blue eyes were so alike, shining with the same loathing. He looked away first, turning to pour three glasses of brandy and shoving one beneath her nose so she had no choice but to accept it. Frederic drained his and poured himself another, while Pemberton seated himself in the other armchair and sipped at the drink, his gaze contemplative as he studied Evelyn. His unabashed stare rankled, and she found her skin covered with gooseflesh, but she forced herself to focus.

Her brother broke the silence; rude as ever. "Spit it out, Evelyn, before you choke on it." Without a chair left to sit on, Frederic leaned his weight back on his desk in affected nonchalance.

The brandy burned her throat with the first swallow, but the second sent warmth through her and nestled down in her belly. It gave her something resembling courage. She took a bigger sip.

"I overheard you this morning, speaking of something impossible. Marrying me off…"

"Skulking about in the hallways now, like a nosy servant?"

It was the drink talking, she knew, but the venom in his voice unsettled her still. He had been detached and uninvolved for years, but never cruel.

"Well, brother. You were, as always, far too loud," she said in a soft voice.

An indolent summer breeze stirred the curtain in front of the open window and they all turned, attention caught by the movement. The Duke wore a faint smirk, as if their bickering was nothing but a diverting pastime to him, and his fingers danced on the arm of his chair. Evelyn wished he would leave. If he had any manners at all he would have excused himself, but he seemed enjoyed things like this. She supposed she should be grateful to him for calling Frederic off.

"Frederic," she began again, but he interrupted her.

"It is your duty to marry, Evelyn." Frederic shrugged. "Did you think you could live out your days as a spinster in my home, playing with the ponies?"

It was a sharp, poignant hit. She took another swallow of the brandy, searching for more of that golden courage it had lent her. "This is my home too," she said weakly.

"Father is dead. I am The Marquess now. It is not your home; it is mine."

"And I am still in mourning, Frederic, though I see you have given up the *charade* of having a heart. Did you love father at all?"

Frederic drained his glass and poured another.

Evelyn's lip tightened at the drinking, but instead of speaking of it, she gestured at his flippant clothing, flamboyant as a pink's. "Is that the sort of thing Adele prefers?"

"Do not speak of her again, I warn you." Frederic pushed off from the desk as if to threaten her a second time, but the Duke stood with sudden violence.

He did not speak, only stood in tight-lipped silence until Frederic reclined back on the desk as if it had been his intention all along to do so. Pemberton scoffed and turned away to read the titles of the books on the shelves as if he were alone in the library. His fingers tapped the spines as if to music. Evelyn watched the Duke, forgetting her brother for a moment. Even with his rumpled, slip shod appearance, he was a fine figure. Why wouldn't he be? He was a Duke. She did not like the way he cowed

Frederic with a glance and stepped in to fight for her as if she needed his assistance. If he felt her glare on him, his only response was that selfsame smirk.

"Who is he?" Evelyn asked.

"Who?" Frederic said.

"Do not be dense, Frederic." Evelyn rubbed her temples with her free hand. The brandy had gone from her stomach to her head.

"A marquess, which is more than you deserve—the way you treat me. You are not my mother," said Frederic, jabbing a finger at her. "You may not censor my behavior."

"Which marquess?" She began to name them all in her mind, discarding the ones she knew to be married. Her heart sped up, a hummingbird's wings in her chest. "Who is he?"

Frederic's glee was evident in his features. Perhaps the man was excessively wealthy, and he was hoping for an allowance from her future husband. She would never allow it. Supplying Frederic with money was the same as supporting his unhealthy habits and sending him to an early grave. Or perhaps Frederic was just joyful at her discomfort— neither option would surprise her now.

"The Marquess of Ashwood."

Pemberton clicked his tongue. Evelyn racked her brain for the face to put to the name. Lord Ashwood.

"No!" Evelyn gasped. "You would not, Frederic; he is far too old for me. Why he's older than father!"

"Some women would consider that a favorable thing," Pemberton said, his nose tucked in a book. "Old men are far more likely to leave a wealthy widow in a timely fashion." He looked up at her and gave a sly wink. "While you are still young enough to enjoy life, you know."

With his gaze fixed again on the page in front of him, he could not see Evelyn's mouth widening in horror at his words.

"What a crude thing to say," she said. "You are both despicable and I see now why you have become fast friends. Please remember, that the *Ton* will forgive a Duke, what they will not forgive a marquess."

Frederic sputtered. "She censures you now," he said to his friend, but the Duke only laughed and the sound of that laugh touched something deep in the pit of her belly. She didn't like it--Not one bit.

Evelyn rose from her chair, intending to storm from the room, but the drink made her sway. She caught herself on the shelf and a moment later Pemberton was at her elbow. He steadied her. For a breath, with his face so close to hers, her only thought was how handsome he was. A breath later, she came back to her sense. Evelyn clutched at her anger through the cloud of alcohol induced indifference as if it was all that could save her.

"Let me go!" She wrenched herself from his grip and although tipsy, she managed to set her glass on the table. She wanted to fling it into her brother's face, but of course, they had no crystal to waste.

Evelyn stormed from the room and slammed the door closed on her brother's string of expletives and the Duke's raucous laughter. It sent shivers through her.

3

Lady Evelyn spent the evening in her rooms, wishing the effects of the drink would wear off a bit faster. She had never indulged so before. Of course, she drank the clarets and punches served at social functions, but always sipped with moderation as the evening progressed, and on a stomach full of rich food to dull the rush. Losing control irritated her. A knock at the door announced the arrival of a tea tray.

"Leave it there," Evelyn said to her lady's maid, Bess.

Bess placed the tray on Evelyn's secretary and began to arrange a plate.

"Bess." Evelyn tugged at her rumpled hair, pulled from the pins with careless haste. "Do you think the Duke is handsome?"

"Any woman with eyes would find the Duke handsome, my Lady," Bess said, with a coy sort of smile. "But he is not the sort that makes an easy husband, I imagine. Always chasing after the next pretty thing, that one. Just what I hear, of course. Pardon, my Lady."

"Of course," Evelyn mumbled, but she was stuck on the memory Pemberton's face so close to hers she could see the scar above his eye. She wondered where he had gotten it from. A fight? A fall from a horse? Anything seemed possible, from him.

"Will that be all, my Lady?" Bess asked, by the door.

Evelyn nodded and she was left alone again. She lay back on her bed in the mounds of downy blankets, looking up at the gauzy canopy above her bed until she drifted to sleep. When she woke, the tea had gone cold but her head was clear. With the clarity came a plan and Evelyn was in a hurry to enact it. With the pull of a bells ring she summoned Bess and the maid set to work on her hair.

Evelyn dressed for dinner in a deep violet muslin gown that was suitable for half mourning. It had been almost a year since her father's death and she had yet to don bright colors or extravagant fabrics. Evelyn was not even sure what the fashions were this Season; not that she could afford anything new. She sighed as she entered the family dining room.

Pemberton was at the table beside her brother. Frederic must have invited him to stay the evening, or perhaps the week; as if they could afford to entertain.

"Lady Evelyn," the Duke said, rising.

"Your Grace," she said, nodding in acknowledgment for him to sit. Frederic did not so much as look up at her entrance. "Good evening, gentlemen."

"I thought the brandy would have kept you abed," Frederic slurred. "Shame it did not."

"You are not so lucky as that. Of course, if you were lucky at all, we might not be in such debt from your gambling." She flashed him a blithe smile and accepted the offer of jellied duck from the footman. "Speaking of your poor decisions, why do you not marry a wealthy woman and make amends for your own mistakes?"

Frederic and the Duke stared at her, shocked at her bald language. Then, the Duke laughed. "*Touché*, Evermont!"

Evelyn did not respond. Her brother's face was turning an alarming shade of purple.

"Gads, she has a mouth on her!" Pemberton continued. He looked delighted. "I have never seen you anything but prim and proper, restrained to a fault."

"I will marry none other than my love, Adele. To do otherwise would be to tear my heart into a thousand pieces." Frederic interjected.

"You cannot marry an actress!" Evelyn was aghast at the suggestion. "Good heavens, can you imagine what that would do for our reputation? And here, I did not think it could get any worse!"

"Best I marry you off then, before our reputation is entirely in tatters," Frederic said.

"Why are you doing this? You are the problem. You should fix it. Marry an heiress."

"To marry any other than Adele seems the cruelest kind of torture!"

"I see the drama of the theater is rubbing off on you." Evelyn shook her head, amazed at his hypocrisy. "And yet you have no qualms marrying me off without even the potential for love?"

Pemberton tilted his glass at her, as if she had earned a point, but her brother still refused to see reason. If he could see anything at all, being blind-drunk as he was.

"If you have a heart, Evelyn, it is only for the horses. Do not pretend you have ever held a man in half as much affection as you have those beasts."

The remark stung with its truthfulness. She had every woman's wish of marrying a man she loved, but she had never found a man that ignited true passion within her. Perhaps the fault was with her. When her retort was not forthcoming, the men went back to prattling on about their latest club. The food tasted dull in her mouth. Every scrape of fork and knife against the plate grated on her ears. There had to be something she could do, she would not marry that man. "I will see to it, that my husband will not advance you one thin farthing," she said.

"*Touché*," Pemberton said again.

She glared at him, but refrained from chastising the Duke and telling him to mind his own business. "Frederic," she said at last, trying to force her tone into sweetness. "Perhaps you could arrange a dinner at Evermont, a to-do of sorts."

"Why would I do that?" he asked.

Frederic abhorred polite company, for they did not engage in any of the reckless, self-endangering behaviors he found so stimulating of late.

"So that I may meet potential suitors. You do not need to limit me to this man, whom I have never met and is old enough to be my father. Allow me find a husband of my own." Evelyn was begging, she knew, but she could not help herself. If she was forced to be married, at least let her have a choice in the man she would be wed to. Surely she could find someone she could respect. "I promise not to dally in my selection, but let me choose."

"Really, Evelyn, do not sound so desperate. It is unbecoming."

"It is not a terrible idea, my friend, what harm can it do?" The Duke asked. He was eyeing her with that predatory gaze again. "A dinner would be a fine enough way to spend an evening."

"Please, with the bores of the *Ton* all around me, and no escape because I have invited them into my own home? No."

"Oh, Frederic, you are being cruel! What can it hurt?" Evelyn cried.

This seemed the final straw, for Frederic flung himself from his chair and slammed his fists down on the table. The vase in the center of the table upended, spilling water across the tablecloth. Evelyn tried to save the expensive vase, but it toppled off of the table and shattered.

"We cannot host a dinner party, sister mine, because no one would attend. There, are you pleased with yourself? Dragging that admission out of me must delight your nasty little temper."

Evelyn pushed back from the table to avoid the cascading water.

"What... what are you saying?"

He shook his head at her, eyes wide in dramatic

fashion as if he thought her a dullard. "I am saying that the *Ton* will have nothing to do with us."

The Duke, who sat out of range of the flood waters, was tapping his fingers on the side of his wine glass. Footmen converged to clean the mess away.

"B-because of father's death? That's absurd."

That did seem absurdly cold, even for the Peerage. Her brother was a bachelor and a marquess. Even with his reputation, there should be women clamoring to marry him. Frederic only shook his head at her again, muttered an expletive under his breath, and left the room, unheeding that he was leaving his sister unchaperoned with an unmarried man.

Evelyn and the Duke of Pemberton were alone in the room. Drops of water made quiet plops as they hit the ground.

"I am afraid your family's reputation is rather in the black at the moment, Lady Evelyn," said the Duke. "Your brother is, understandably, touchy about the subject."

"But, what happened? I know he gambles but, so do most men!"

The Duke hesitated, seeming to weigh his words before he said them. "His indiscretions have been rather more... overt, than society would deem polite. Suffice it to say, he has burned many bridges with his debts and his behavior, and the Evermont name is not as prestigious as it once was. My apologies."

He turned to go. It was the first time she had ever seen the collected man so unsettled.

"Wait. Your Grace, please."

Up close his rumpled appearance seemed intentional.

His hair was tousled, jacket unbuttoned, and his cravat loosed.

"Yes?"

They were almost as close as that moment in the study, when he had touched her. If he thought there would be more of that here, he was wrong. Evelyn arranged her face into a stern countenance to quash any impertinent ideas he might be having.

"I have a proposition for you," she said and she felt the heat of a blush on her pale skin as he raised an eyebrow. "I mean, an idea, of something we might do together."

She could tell it was coming out all wrong when the smirk on the Duke's face only grew more wicked with every word. She would slap him if he were not a Duke and if she did not need his assistance.

"Do go on. I am most intrigued now," Pemberton drawled.

Evelyn's eyes caught on that little scar. The hairs of his eyebrow split around the puckered skin. She wanted to reach up and smooth them down for they were as unruly as the man himself. He raised his fingers to it, in what would be a self-conscious gesture on anyone else.

"It is nothing like *that*." She moved a safer distance away. "You keep a stable, do you not?"

Evelyn stood beside the hearth. It had been brushed clean and the firewood rack was filled with a neat stack of decorative birch logs. The Duke's reply, when it came, was closer than she had expected.

"I do, a fine one at that. Fastest horses in Norfolk." He

rested one hand on the mantle and angled his body toward hers.

"And would you care to put a wager on that?"

Pemberton raised his eyebrows. His face lost the perpetual arrogance, but the mask was back a moment later. He gave her a wry grin that did unpleasant things to her stomach. Why did she let him affect her so?

"I would indeed," Pemberton said. "But my dear, I know the state of your finances. You have nothing to wager."

"That is my concern. I have funds of my own."

"You seemed a prudent girl prior to this evening." He grinned at her. "I prefer this new version, the kind that smashes vases and makes unwise bets."

"Charming, but I do not prefer you at all. Are we agreed then?"

"On your head be it." He shrugged. "What are the conditions?"

"A match race, on turf."

The Duke named his bet. It was a sum that struck her dumb.

"Do not tell me you are getting cold feet already. What happened to that fierce pride in your horses? You were so confident only a moment ago."

She knew it was foolish, but his mockery needled her. All she wanted was to wipe the smug look off his face when her horse won, and she knew her horse would win.

"What is this?" Frederic had returned.

"I thought you had gone to bed," said Evelyn.

"As you can plainly see, I did not. What is it you two were discussing?"

The Duke's Wicked Wager

Evelyn shifted. "It is not your business."

"You are embarrassed about it. Look at her, red as an apple!" Frederic hooted in delight. "Have you been flirting with my sister, Pemberton?"

"We have arranged a little race for tomorrow," the Duke said. "With a small wager, just for the excitement."

Frederic tutted. "My pristine sister, placing bets? Naughty. Well, I want in as well."

"Absolutely not," Evelyn said, even as the Duke said. "On who?"

"Your horse, of course," Frederic replied to the Duke. "I am not a fool."

"Good chap." Pemberton clapped Frederic on the shoulder.

"No!" Evelyn cried. Frederic betting would offset her own and it all would be for nothing.

"Off to bed now, or you will be sleeping through the race," Pemberton urged her brother.

Frederic, to Evelyn's surprise, did as the Duke suggested and retired to his rooms.

"Why did you do that? He has not got a coin to spend! You bring out the very worst in him."

"Cheer up. Now you have a chance to win twice what you had before, both from me and your brother."

"As if my brother would pay me a cent of it, and he is already in debt. And I cannot afford to pay him out if I lose!"

"If you lose, I shall pay him off myself. Let him have his fun, Lady Evelyn, he has little enough of it in his life."

Evelyn threw her hands in the air at that. "Yes, poor Frederic. But I do not want your charity."

"Every kindness is not charity," said the Duke.

"I do not know you well, not even at all, in fact, but I suspect your kindness comes with many strings attached." Evelyn stepped close, and this time she did not tremble at the nearness of him. "I do not like strings, but will not matter. My horse will win. Goodnight, Your Grace."

His eyes followed her as she swept out of the room and she wished it did not feel so much like fleeing.

4

Evelyn buried her face in her pillows. Why was she dreaming of the Duke of Pemberton? George Pender was a terrible rake, a senseless man. He also was a terribly handsome, and his deep laugh, cut through her and made her flustered. At least she was aware how foolish her desires were and therefore would not succumb to them. There were more important things to worry about today and her nerves were alight with anticipation. Bess helped Evelyn dress in a somber charcoal grey dress and pulled her hair into a tight chignon.

Dawn was just beginning to bloom on the horizon as she went down to breakfast. Always an early riser, she enjoyed the quiet solitude of breakfast, alone in the parlor with birdsong for company. This morning, however, the Duke was already seated at the table. He was reading a book; the title obscured by his hand. He did not stand. He did not even look up as she entered.

"Good morning, Lady Evelyn."

Realizing she was standing stupefied in the doorway, she hurried inside the breakfast parlor and hesitated before she took a seat. He was sitting in her usual chair.

"Good morning."

Evelyn fidgeted. She could hardly see the sunrise from her seat. "I confess I did not expect to see you awake so early, given your indulgences at dinner."

"I prefer early mornings to late nights."

"I would not have guessed that," she said, pouring herself a cup of tea from the steaming pot.

"We hardly know each other," he said, looking up from his book at last. "You may assume any manner of things about me, and I about you, but that does not make any of them true."

"Oh. Hmm, indeed." She was caught off guard by the whole encounter and annoyed by the disruption to her routine.

They said no more, eating breakfast in silence — he with his book and she with her thoughts. Frederic would not arise for hours yet, of that much she could be certain. Evelyn had just finished her plate of cut fruit when a horse's shrill whinny split the silence, a stallion giving challenge to the other stallion in the yard.

"Ah, Kingston has arrived." Pemberton dog-eared the page and set the book down.

At the window, he pulled the curtain back and smiled at the sight. She reached over and unfolded the abused page, sliding a napkin between to hold his place, then rose to see the horse for herself. Kingston was tall, a full hand taller than her pick for the race. His tail flagged as he pranced and snorted.

"Grey is my favorite color." He was looking at her as he said it. "Steady. Quiet grace. I sent one of your footmen to my estate last night, to alert the grooms and bring Kingston here this morning. I hope you do not mind."

"Not at all," she said. "He looks young."

"Just three. I find they are full of spirit at that age."

She made a skeptical sound. "I prefer them older. More time to mature. A muscular horse is a faster horse, and the training time is important as well. An older steadier horse will be more responsive to the rider."

"Is that so?" he asked and she blushed, feeling as if he was not talking about horses. "Personally, I trust in instinct and blood," he continued. "The blood will out. Horses who want to run, run, and they run faster than the horse beside them when they are given a challenge. They have no need for human instruction, which will only impede their natural inclination."

"Instinct only takes them so far."

"That is the most splendid thing about these sorts of contests. We will be able to prove this very afternoon which one of our philosophies is the most successful."

"Indeed, Your Grace."

"Are you not the slightest bit concerned, Lady Evelyn? It is your future we are betting on."

Evelyn folded her hands just before her waist. She would not waver now.

"Shall we head to the barns? I confess, I am eager to get on."

Pemberton offered his arm, and she accepted with a

tight nod. Kingston and his entourage of three, a rider and two grooms, followed them to the stables where she had one of her staff show them to the empty wing. The Duke went with his horse while Evelyn sought her stable master.

"Is Diadem ready, then?" Evelyn asked Stanton.

His balding head was dipping low over the page before him. He looked up in surprise when Evelyn entered the room.

"Oh yes, my Lady. I believe young Thomas is with her now." He got up from his chair and followed her out into the barn. "She knows something exciting is happening today. I've never seen her so worked up!"

"Have you marked the track with a flag for the finish and the start?"

"Not yet. Care for a walk?"

When they returned from their walk of the race's course, Frederic was waiting in the stable. He had bathed and dressed, but the drink from last night had not yet worn off or he was already in his cups at breakfast.

"Is it starting?" he asked Evelyn as she walked past him.

He would not follow her into the stables, not with his absurd fear of horses.

Over her shoulder she replied, "In a moment. But hurry along to the track or you might be trampled."

She had Diadem brought out well in advance of Kingston. The stallion's prancing would upset the more delicate mare and she wanted her calm and collected. Despite the Duke's insistence, pure adrenaline was not enough to make a fine racehorse.

"Hold her back at the start, Charles," she instructed Diadem's rider as she glanced at Kingston's sweat covered flanks. "She will want to keep stride with Kingston, but let the colt burn himself out, then strike."

Evelyn gave the horse a final pat and went to take her place on the rail beside Pemberton and Frederic.

"Are you certain you want to continue with this wager," the Duke asked, giving her one last chance to bow out gracefully. "A mare against a stallion is a poor choice."

"I am certain," she said.

A moment later, Stanton began the race with a shot from his pistol.

Kingston broke from the start with all the exuberance she had expected. He tossed his head at the lightest touch on the rein from the rider's hands, refusing to listen to any instruction. The horse wanted only to run. He was fast, she had to give him that, but he was also covered in sweat, his gray coat, almost black with it. Diadem was four lengths back. Her ears were flat along her neck, pricked to listen to her rider. She was waiting, biding her time until she was asked to fly.

"Not yet," Evelyn whispered. Pemberton glanced at her from the corner of his eye.

"What was that?"

"Nothing, Your Grace."

The horses rounded the bend and Kingston was beginning to flag or Diadem's rider gave the mare her head, and the mare's heart nearly burst for the speed she poured on. The distance between the two was closing rapidly. Diadem stretched her neck out, arrow straight over the turf. Evelyn could almost feel the violent lurching of the horse beneath her, the thud of her hooves, the clumps of grass flying up beside her face. The Duke leaned against the rail beside her, as if he could will his horse forward. Frederic chanted Kingston's name behind them.

Diadem was neck and neck with Kingston now. The stallion was covered in sweat as the jockey urged him on. The mare was straining, veins popping out on her neck as she fought to pass the stallion, but once she caught up, Evelyn knew then she had won it. Once Diadem was side by side with the other horse, there was no stopping her. She hated being second and in a moment she had pulled ahead by a nose. Then by a neck.

"What a fine mare she is!" Pemberton cheered, with no hint of anger. "And I had thought the big gray was your best."

"Bellona," Evelyn said with a smile. The gray filly was one of her favorites too.

Then, it happened. Diadem stumbled. It all happened in a flash, the jockey flying over the mare's ears and Diadem crashing to the ground, unable to catch herself at the incredible speed she had built.

"No!" Evelyn ducked beneath the fence, picked up her skirts and ran to the mare.

"Lady Evelyn, wait!" The Duke ran after her.

Diadem was on the ground, struggling to rise. Charles, blessedly, was unharmed. His clothes were streaked with grass and dirt stains but he was more concerned for the mare. Kingston continued to run on in the distance, fighting against his rider's attempts to pull him up. The race was finished, regardless. He had won. The Duke caught hold of Evelyn's hand.

"Let me go!" She yanked away from him; all thought of the bet had flown from her mind when Diadem went down.

"She may thrash and kick out. Let me help her," he said, with a voice that brooked no arguments. "Mind for once, Lady Evelyn. You are not the only one here who cares."

But Evelyn shook off his hand and ran for her mare. By the time Evelyn reached her, Diadem was on her feet. She shook with pain and tossed her head. She refused to put weight on her front right leg and Evelyn felt for heat running a hand down the leg. The Duke scowled at Evelyn, but she ignored the glare and continued to feel Diadem's leg, searching for the problem.

"She is quite calm now, Your Grace, I hardly think she will kick out when she is tired and hurt."

The leg was hot to touch due to the race itself and Diadem tossed her head, annoyed with Evelyn's prodding. She was unable to tell what if anything had caused the fall.

"We should take her to the stable." Pemberton took the mare by the reins and led her away from the track.

Kingston had pulled up at last and his rider dismounted. He was having a devil of a time dealing with the unruly stallion on the ground as well, and the Duke sent a second groom off to help him. Frederic stepped back as they passed as if the limping mare would run him down. Evelyn walked by her man Charles without a word.

In the barn, Stanton was waiting with two of the grooms.

"Hold her steady now, she may not like this." The old man bent to feel her leg, then coaxed the mare to bend it and allow him to look at her hoof. "Oy!"

Evelyn and the Duke peered over Stanton's considerable form.

"Is that a nail in the poor girl's frog?" The Duke stroked Diadem's neck and scratched her head.

"Good heavens!" Evelyn cried. "How? She was checked over this morning, was she not? The blacksmith has not been here in weeks, where could she have picked it up?"

Stanton straightened with a wince. "Looks intentional, my Lady. Hammered in partway, perhaps, so she would not show lameness until the nail was pounded in by the race. Give me the pincers," he told one of the grooms.

Evelyn's mind did not take long to put it all together, and she whirled on the Duke of Pemberton.

"You scoundrel! You rake! You cad! You would ruin a horse for your own gain! You are despicable."

Diadem pinned her ears at the outburst and puffed a nervous snort from her nostrils.

"Begging your pardon?" Pemberton was torn between soothing the mare and the upset young woman. He did a half job on both. "I had nothing to do with this, Lady Evelyn. I am a sportsman, and I enjoy a fair sport, not one I win by default."

"And with so much on the line, you did not think this might tip the scales in your favor?" Evelyn attempted to wrench the reins from his grip and stabbed a finger toward the door. "Go! At once!"

The Duke handed the mare off to the groom to cool her. "I will not be ordered about like a hound," he said, quietly. "I understand you are distraught. I will do everything in my power to get to the bottom of this matter, but I am not at fault and I will not tolerate your accusations."

They faced off. Evelyn's nostrils flared like one of her horses and the Duke's stare was hard and cool, the faint twitch of his scarred eyebrow the only sign of his agitation.

"Very well," she said, looking away.

"Did you see anyone in the barn earlier?" The Duke asked Stanton. "Someone who does not belong here?"

"Your men, of course, Your Grace." Stanton rubbed his bald patch nervously. "The grooms for Kingston and the rider as well."

"My men have no reason to do such a thing. I pay them a fair wage whether the horse wins or not."

"Of course, I did not mean to imply they would," said Stanton, ducking his head and tending to the mare. He pulled out the nail with the pincers and held it up for inspection. "But no, other than The Lord Evermont and my own staff, no one was here this morning."

"Frederic?" Evelyn and the Duke said in unison.

Frederic hated riding. He was awful at it, and had taken a very nasty spill as a young boy that had left him fearful of horses ever since. Though it was most unbecoming in a gentleman.

"I thought it strange, for I cannot say he has come to

the stables since your father's passing, but aye. He was here, and being Lord of the estate, I did not question his reasons." Stanton pursed his lips. "I should walk Diadem to cool," he said. "Regardless of her foot. I will soak it afterwards."

"Yes. Yes of course, Stanton," Evelyn said. "Will you be able to care for her on your own or should I send for aid?"

"We can manage this, my Lady. Get some salts ready," he told the groom. "We will soak the hoof as soon as she is cool. She'll be right as rain soon."

He led the mare away with tender words and Evelyn felt one of the many weights upon her lift. Diadem was in good hands. Now it was time to find the wretch who had harmed her horse and cost her a fortune she could not afford to pay. She wanted to tug at her hair and rip the gloves from her hands. She scowled at the Duke.

"You still believe this is my doing. I can see it plain on your face," Pemberton said. "Not much of a card player, are you?"

"My brother plays enough for the both of us, I think."

The Duke responded only with a grunt. It rankled, the way he brushed aside her concerns. She fell in stride beside him, letting him lead the way out of the barn and down the loose stone path toward the house. The heat of summer was upon them, and in spite of her bonnet she was half-blinded by the intensity of the sun's light. The Duke paid it no mind, as he seemed to disregard any matter that did not interest or benefit him.

Evelyn scowled at his back. His stride was strong,

confident, shoulders straight and blond hair brilliant as gold in the sun.

"Do you disagree?" Evelyn asked. She hurried to keep pace with him. "He tosses away our family's future for an actress and other cheap thrills. He has no regard for me or my prospects, and I cannot change his behavior nor distance myself from him. Is that fair?"

He stopped and spun in a sudden, violent way that drew her up short.

"In truth, I thought your brother's company nothing more than an amusing distraction, and his downward spiral added to the entertainment." The Duke held up a hand to stop her outraged reply. "I see now the destruction it has wrought, for it is hard to turn a blind eye."

"Then why do you enable him so?"

"I thought I was being a friend, a shoulder to lean on in his time of grief. I believed that when his grief lessened, he would bounce back." The Duke tapped his leg in a staccato beat. "It is clear now that is not the case. It was my mistake, and I will do what I can to repair it. Your brother is truly my friend despite what you may believe, Lady Evelyn."

5

They found Frederic in the dining room. His jacket hung on the back of his chair and sweat had soaked through his shirt, revealing the pink of his skin underneath.

"Evermont," the Duke said, with all the disappointment of a father. "Why did you do it?"

Evelyn gasped.

It clicked then, why the Duke had brought them straight to Frederic. He must have put two and two together the moment Stanton had mentioned Frederic's presence in the stable. She was, once again, caught by surprise at the depths of her brother's depravity.

"Do what?" Frederic asked.

"There is no point in denying it," Evelyn said, rounding on her brother. "We know the truth. How could you, Frederic? Diadem is innocent in this. How could you cause her pain?"

He slumped. Whether he did not have the heart or the wit to continue his act, the result was the same.

"Think of it as a compliment," said Pemberton. "He thought your horse so likely to win; he had to sabotage the event to make certain he did not lose his bet."

"I thought there was a chance, at least." Frederic dropped his head into his hands.

"But how did you do it?" his sister asked. "I know you are afraid of horses, and not a skilled enough actor to be faking that."

His reply was muffled by his palms. "I paid a groom to do it."

She bit back an expletive of her own, one that would have made Frederic proud. "Who was it? I will have them dismissed and more beside!"

"Oh not one of yours, Evelyn. They are all loyal as dogs," he said. "One of Pemberton's. The young curly-haired fellow."

The Duke bristled. He clenched his hands into fists at his sides, his fingers as still as she had ever seen them.

"Ronald. He will pay for this mark me." Duke reached for Evelyn's hand. "I am not entirely blameless then, for the groom was in my employ, but be aware he will not be employed long. Forgive me, Lady Evelyn."

His palm was warm. It was pleasant, and unnerving.

"I do." She accepted but pulled her hand free.

"You will have your winnings, Evermont. I agreed to pay your sister's bet, should her horse lose. It is the least I can do, with a traitorous staff member to blame for the loss. Now, excuse me, I must see to the bastard's punishment."

He was gone as quickly as that and Evelyn was alone with her brother. Though he seemed sincere in his remorse, looking as dogged as he did, she could not forgive his actions.

"If you were any gentleman at all, you would refuse that money," Evelyn said to her brother, latching on to her anger. It was a safer emotion than the one she had felt at the Duke's touch. "But you have not even a shred of decency left, I see. Do you brother?"

"Must you always nag? I apologized, so move past it." And, as an afterthought he added. "Will the beast recover?"

"I hope so, or you have cost us one of our most promising racehorses." She laughed. "Not that you care a smidgen for the state of Evermont's bloodlines."

"I would have sold all of the beasts when father died, but I thought it would turn you into an even more miserable living companion than you are now."

"Do you expect a thank you for that kindness?"

He waved a dismissive hand. "My head aches. Leave me. Your nagging makes it worse."

"Your costly and excessive consumption of alcohol is what makes it worse," she argued, but obliged. She wanted to be gone, as well.

Frederic snagged her skirts on her way past him and she stopped before he could rip the fabric with his carelessness.

"Your little infatuation has not gone unnoticed, sister, even by me. Do not embarrass yourself. George is a Duke," he said, and released her.

She refused to dwell on his words. She huffed and

turned to leave. Drunks were delusional and often imagined things while in their cups.

Stanton would have seen Diadem would be tended to by now, so Evelyn went back out to the stable to check her. It would be a shame to see her retired to a broodmare, but if the leg was not fit for racing that was all she could hope for. She closed her eyes collecting herself. This was a disaster.

"It is too soon to tell what the lasting damage will be," Stanton said. He was hovering around the mare's stall. "I pulled the nail and applied a poultice. The boys will see to it she gets a cold sponging on the leg every hour. Tomorrow we will soak it again and reapply the poultice. It will be a week before we know the damage."

"It seems as good a plan as any." Evelyn kissed the mare's velvet nose. "Have you seen the Duke pass this way? He was looking for one of his grooms."

"I did, and sent him in the man's direction, but I would not be in that man's shoes for any sum."

"What do you mean?" Evelyn asked.

"The Duke had a frightening look about him, my Lady. Dark as a storm cloud." Stanton shook his head. "He would be done with that business now, I imagine, and you may find him with Kingston in the paddock."

She did find Pemberton there, stroking his grey stallion. Kingston stood quivering under his master's touch.

"The man has paid for his misdeed," was all the Duke said when she approached.

Evelyn did not want to know more than that. Kingston, realizing his owner's attention had left him, gave the Duke a rude shove with his nose. Pemberton surprised her when he did not strike or reprimand the horse.

"I expect you think he is ill-trained," Pemberton said, inclining his head at the stallion and scratching the boy beneath his chin. "In comparison to yours, I suppose he is."

"You are not a foolish man, Your Grace, so your methods must work or you would change them." She pursed her lips. "They could be improved upon, of course."

"Of course." He held his arm out to her and she laid her hand upon it. They stood for a moment before the big gray stallion and he snuffled Evelyn curiously.

Together, they walked along the paddock. Grey-bottomed clouds encroached upon the blue sky, bringing the threat of a summer thunderstorm.

"Will we back before it begins?" she asked, looking up at the clouds.

"We are not far from the stables. I think we are safe."

They walked along a dirt path cut through the pastures and listened to the droning buzz of insects among the tall grass. Horses lifted their heads in interest at the intruders, but grew bored of the humans' meandering stroll and returned to the more interesting subject of food.

"I have a solution to the matter of the bet," the Duke said.

Her stomach sank. She had forgotten with all the drama of the morning that she now owed the man quite a sizable sum, one she had never expected to have to pay.

"In lieu of paying your agreed upon bet, as you cannot afford it, I will accept your stable in payment. The grooms and other staff will remain, for they will know best how to care for the horses, and truthfully there is no room for even this handful of horses in my stable. It is full to bursting with new foals due any day."

Evelyn stopped. His words were a nightmare come to life and she could not breathe. She wanted to pretend she had not heard, but they hung in the air, needling like a biting fly.

"You sound as if you are offering me a most gracious gift, when in truth you are threatening to take my most prized possession!"

"I believe I am being quite generous. Or do you have a pile of funds secreted away somewhere?"

"No," she said softly.

"I did not think so."

"Even when you attempt to be a gentleman, your true nature is apparent! Any man of respectability would not hold a woman to a bet he knew she could not manage to pay."

"Lady Evelyn, mind your tone. I refuse to back out of a deal, and I respect you far too much to believe you would be comfortable with me doing so. I intend to allow you to visit the stables as you have been, and will take your opinion into account with decisions concerning the horses. It *is* a most gracious offer."

He did not raise his voice, nor stamp about as her brother did when in a mood. His anger was quiet and contained, but far more frightening. Evelyn did not care if he was angry, for she was far angrier and with far more right to be so.

"Kind? Oh indeed. How kind of you to allow me to have input regarding my own horses, my own stable!"

"Before the stable was your brother's; it was your father's," he said. "It has never been yours, Lady Evelyn." His words stung like sweat in a wound. "Nor will it be."

She knew he was right. The thought rankled, but it was true. She raised her chin a little and stared him down, but he didn't look away and she began to feel her eyes water with frustrated tears.

"I think you have been indulged by the men in your life thus far. The truth is, a mare cannot stand against a stallion even if she is strong and full of heart."

"She was hurt," Evelyn protested.

"So she was," the Duke said softly.

"And Frederic is not punished at all for this, it is only I who suffers," she said. "After all he won with his deceit this morning, but he cannot spare a bit of compassion for his sister."

"This is for the best," the Duke said. "As your brother proved, he has no love for the horses."

"No. And no compassion," Lady Evelyn agreed. "But you are both horrible!"

"I shall escort you back to the house now, so you may

settle yourself." This time, his arm was not an offer, but a demand. She took it, knowing she looked petulant and childish, and they walked back to the manor in silence.

6
———

It was only after a long bath and a hot cup of tea that she felt well enough to go downstairs. Bess had curled Evelyn's hair and left ringlets loose to frame her face while the rest was twisted up and pinned behind a ribbon. Evelyn paired it with another charcoal grey dress and pearls. The colors exaggerated her pale complexion, but she liked the effect of the monochromatic palette.

"It is fair, I know that Bess," Evelyn said, dabbing apple scented perfume onto her wrist. "More than fair, but I do not want him to feel as though he owns me now as well."

"He sees how your brother has treated you, my Lady. He wants to take care of you, and the horses. Surely there are worse things than that?"

"Surely." Evelyn straightened the jars on her vanity and laid her brush down in its place between them. "If it were anyone except the Duke…"

"Because you have feelings for him?"

Evelyn turned with such vigor she bumped the vanity and jostled all of her possessions out of place again. Bess laughed.

"I do not!" Evelyn protested.

"Everyone else can see it, my Lady. Even The Lord Evermont." Bess bent to pick a silver comb up from the floor.

"It does not matter," Evelyn said at last. "He is a Duke, Bess. He has his pick of ladies. He will not pick the shrewish sister of his near beggared best friend."

"Then perhaps, the sister should not be so shrewish," Bess said, and Evelyn frowned at her. It was not seemly for a lady's maid to speak so to her mistress, but Evelyn did not reprimand her. Bess had been one of the few people she could speak to this past year. Flustered, she did not reply at all.

***

FREDERIC AND PEMBERTON were playing a hand of cards when she went down to the parlor and their boisterous laughter filled the room. Her subtle apple fragrance was drowned by the smell of smoke and spice and brandy.

"Lady Evelyn," the Duke said, laying down his hand and standing to greet her. His voice set her heart to racing.

Did she care for him? If so, it had happened without her notice. She could not deny the flip of her stomach when he smiled at her.

"Your Grace," she said. "May we speak?"

"Of course. Evermont, do you mind?"

Frederic shot Evelyn a withering glare. He slapped his cards down onto the playing table and skulked out of the room, once again leaving her alone with the Duke. In his half-drunken oblivious state Frederic was either unaware of the impropriety, or he just didn't care. She ignored her brother, and moved to the corner of the parlor where a chessboard was set out with a half-played game. The white player was being beaten soundly.

"I accept your offer," said Evelyn. "And I apologize for my rudeness earlier. It was unseemly." She fingered the scalloped crown of the black queen. The white queen lay taken.

"It was a chance to see a chink in that pristine armor of yours," the Duke said. "I enjoyed it."

"You would." Evelyn slid an ivory pawn forward. "Though you will own the stable on paper, I expect all decisions will go through me. I know what is best for those horses. I have seen some of them foaled."

The Duke clasped his hand over hers before she could lift it from the piece.

"There is no saving that game," he said. "Your brother is a terrible chess player. Nearly as awful at the game as he is at cards."

She looked up at him, at his slightly crooked nose and scarred eyebrow, and slight smile. "Perhaps the best option is to surrender, then."

He pressed her back against the petite table, almost touching his body to hers. The motion jostled the chess table and sent pieces skittering across the smooth surface of the board. Evelyn gasped in surprise, but he held her hands in his until she stilled.

"Is it so dreadful to give up control?" he asked, his voice a soft rumble against her ear that rode down into her belly. The moment held as his deep blue eyes bored into hers. She could smell the brandy and the smoke, and something else underneath, a scent that was particularly male. She felt her lips part of their own accord.

"I do not surrender easily" She whispered into that stillness. Her voice trembled.

"I do like a challenge," he said.

She slid her hand free from his and reached up to touch the scar above his eye. The skin was velvet smooth beneath her finger. It was a brief but heady moment. When he stepped away, her fingertips seemed to tingle, protesting the absence of him. Evelyn ducked away from him and turned to face the window. Her heart was racing.

"Do not marry Lord Ashwood," the Duke said.

She faced him, arms crossed over her chest as if it would provide armor against his advances.

"And why should I not?"

He adjusted the cuffs of his shirt. "Because I have asked you not to; because he is so damnably old, and because your brother is a fool."

"I must. We have no means," she said softly.

"Not every man needs an heiress," he said.

"Whatever do you mean?"

"Must you have an explanation for everything in your life?"

The pieces of the chessboard were in disarray. Dark and light wooden figures mingled and Evelyn itched to set them right, back onto their respective squares. She picked up the fallen white queen and sat her on her color.

"Yes. I like order, and certainty. I like having explanations," she said softly. "And if you are planning on keeping company with me, Your Grace, you will need to accept that," Evelyn said. "If you think I am one of your light skirts to jump at your whim, you are solely mistaken." She felt the fire of embarrassment flush her face, but she didn't look away.

The Duke grabbed the black king and queen from their prone positions and placed them with deliberate care onto their squares.

"If you think I would put up with such sass from a light skirt," the Duke said, with a smile for her alone. "You are sorely mistaken."

When he looked at her like that she could not still her swiftly beating heart.

"Shall we play?" he asked gesturing to the board.

"Yes. I would like that," she said meeting his eyes.

Part 2

Promise Me Daring

7

Diadem leapt the fallen tree with ease. The solid, hip high obstruction was no trouble at all for the willing mare. Evelyn reined her up on the far side of the log and leaned down to give the mare's neck a pat. Summer was drawing to an end and the days were cooler with the promise of autumn. For Lady Evelyn Evering, it could not come soon enough.

The beginning of autumn marked the start of the hunting season and the start of Diadem's real training. While the mare had recovered from the nail in her hoof, she would never be racing fit again. It had been a devastating realization, but Evelyn refused to wallow in self-pity and had set herself the task of training Diadem into a quality fox hunter.

The mare had taken to it at once. She had shown no fear in the forest, even alone. Some horses would spook and fret over every little noise in the underbrush and those horses had no potential for hunting, when the pace was fast a startled horse could throw a rider. Evelyn loosened the reins. Diadem dropped her head and made her own way down the trail, picking her hooves up over the gnarled roots. It had been too long since Evelyn had ridden through the forest that blanketed the outskirts of the Evermont acreage. Once the Duke of Pemberton, had returned to his own estate, she found herself with far too much free time.

She thought of the Duke often. She and George Pender had shared only one embrace. It was but one brief moment in the gaming parlor. If he had told Frederic of it, her brother had not reacted in any visible manner. No, her brother, the self-important Marquess of Evermont was just as awful as ever.

"Shall we head home, girl?" Evelyn asked of the mare, who flicked one ear back in interest. "It will be dark soon." Evelyn cast about her eyes searching the nearby tress, but she appeared to have left her groom somewhat behind. It was just as well. Patrick was fearful of her jumping Diadem. Saying it was far too dangerous for a lady, and side saddles were not safe for such things. But Lady Evelyn had been riding since she was a small girl; she knew how to hold her seat.

Evelyn turned Diadem around. She was in no hurry to be home but did not want to be caught out after the sun set. They took a circuitous route around a log. Diadem's leg was prone to swelling if pushed too hard, and she wanted the mare to be ready for a lawn meet in the upcoming weeks – If Frederic agreed to it. He might she thought, if the Duke was on her side about it.

Pemberton held far more sway over her brother's decisions than she ever had. Would Frederic invite the actress he was courting? Adele was her name, a French woman. Now that would cause a scandal. Knowing Frederic and the Duke, the scandal would be half the reason she would be invited. The men found the ruffling of polite society's feathers an amusing spectacle.

She doubted very much that the woman could ride. An actress could not afford to keep a horse, nor would she have any space to ride it. Frederic carried on about how beautiful Adele was, how angelic. Perhaps the Duke found her beautiful as well. That thought rankled. Evelyn comforted herself with the knowledge that an actress could never be anything more than a dalliance for a member of the Peerage, particularly for a Duke.

"Ease up, girl" Evelyn said, tightening her hands lightly on Diadem's reins slowing her.

They had reached a brook almost gone dry in the summer drought. A thin trickle of water wove between pebbles and sticks on the muddy bed. The gap was nearly a meter across, but the banks were steep and treacherous with loose sand. Evelyn gathered up the reins and circled the mare around, bringing her some ten paces back from the brook. Then, she tapped her single spur against the horse's side and the mare burst into a canter. Three paces from the brook, two... Evelyn gathered the horse's mane in her gloved hands and cued Diadem for the jump with the crop; squeezing the pommel between her legs. The mare surged easily over the brook, landing on the other side with a spirited toss of her head.

"They will not be able to touch us, Diadem, we will fly!" Evelyn reached forward and patted the horse's neck. She was in high spirits on the journey home; Patrick would just have to catch her up.

When Diadem broke free from the cover of golden trees Evelyn saw the sky had gone purple and grey above them. Without the sun for guidance, Evelyn could not be sure how much time had passed since she had taken Diadem in the woods. Stanton, the stable master hurried out from the stable to meet her.

"Just in time, my Lady," Stanton said, holding the mare's reins for Evelyn to dismount. "We are in for a storm. Did you lose, Patrick again?"

"He's just behind me," she said as she took Stanton's offered hand, unhooked her front leg and slid from the saddle. She smoothed her riding habit. Diadem turned her head to nuzzle Evelyn's sides, looking for the bites of apple she often received as a reward for a good ride.

"In a moment," Evelyn scolded the pushy mare.

She pulled her hat from her head and tucked it beneath her arm, mindful of its feathers. Her hair was slick with sweat and she was grateful that the Duke was not at the manor to see her in such a state. Thunder threatened, rumbling overhead in a distant murmur.

"I have had all the horses brought in from the pastures." Stanton informed her. Having already pulled the saddle and blanket from Diadem's back, he turned loosening the bridle and replaced it with a halter.

"You should hurry back to the manor before it begins, my Lady."

"I do suppose," Evelyn agreed, but made no move to

The Duke's Wicked Wager

leave. She stood scratching the mare between the ears. Diadem dropped her head to accommodate the woman's reach. "She was wonderful out there. Fearless girl," Evelyn said.

"I'm not surprised, she is one of Valiant's get after all," said Stanton. "But how will she fare in the madness of a hunt?"

"I hope to test that in the next week or two, if Frederic will agree to it." Evelyn sighed. "And the Duke, of course."

Stanton began to brush the sweat from the mare's back. "He has not yet changed a thing about the way the place is run, my Lady."

Though the stable master's words were true, the situation bothered her. Her thoughts of late were torn between the Duke himself and how to buy back the stable from him. The amount of money required was frightening. He might not sell it back to the Evermont estate even if she and her brother could afford it. No, he might keep it just to irritate her. Another rumble of thunder rolled over head, louder now.

"I know you are right, but I do not have to like it," Evelyn said. She slipped a chunk of apple from the pocket of her habit and fed the mare her hard-earned treat. "I should go."

The next peal of thunder was an ear-splitting crack. Evelyn fit her hat back on top of her head, scooped her skirt up by its loop to raise the hem, and ran for home just as Patrick trotted up on his mount. If she had left the stables only a moment earlier, she would have made it. As it was, the clouds released their bounty, with enough vigor that she was drenched by the time she reached the entrance way. The water was warm, at least.

"Good Lord," said Frederic. "You look liked a drowned rat."

Her brother was as helpful as ever.

"Thank you, Frederic. Perhaps you ought to step outside and have a bath yourself; I believe I can smell you from here. Whiskey? You have at last ridded us of our brandy, then. Job well done. Quite an accomplishment."

She did not want to deal with him now. Drenched and dirty from her ride, she wanted nothing more than a lengthy bath and a comfortable chair from which to watch the storm. It battered at the windows with a ferocity that almost drowned out her brother's words.

"Be prepared for dinner in two hours," he said. "I have matters to discuss with you."

He left, abruptly heading toward the parlor. Evelyn's curiosity was peaked. Her brother never wanted to dine with her, and he certainly never had anything to speak with her about. Since her father died, they were like strangers living in the same house. What could have happened?

She hurried up the stairs to find a filled bath already waiting for her; steam slowly curling upwards from the tub.

"Bess, you are a saint." She told her ladies maid in thanks.

With Bess' help, Evelyn pulled the soaked clothes from her body, though they put up a good fight, and sank nose deep into the hot water. The fireplace cast flickering light onto the white and gilt walls. She could see it dance through her closed eyelids.

"I knew you would be out there with those horses until the rain forced you in," said Bess, coming from one of the side rooms with a tray of soap. "And your brother asked the kitchen to cook a proper dinner, so I suspected you would need to dress."

"What is that about, I wonder?" Evelyn mused as she selected a soap with a cheery orange scent. Bits of peel puckered the surface. "Frederic loathes dining with me. He claims I take it as an opportunity to nag."

"Pray he never marries, then, if he cannot bear a bit of nagging." Bess said with a chuckle.

"I do not nag!"

"Of course not, dear." Bess laid out a clean flannel for Evelyn to dry off with.

She bit her lip, a sign she had something to say she did not think Evelyn would like to hear.

"Oh Bess what is it?" Evelyn said, frowning.

"Your mourning period will be over soon," said Bess, studying the carpet. "Shall I have your other dresses brought out and freshened up?"

Had it been so long? Evelyn could hardly believe a year had passed since her fiancé had been killed and her father had slipped away in his sleep, with as little warning as a lightning strike. The somber colors were a daily reminder.

"I suppose we should, since Frederic expects me to begin entertaining suitors." Suitors like Lord Ashwood. The man was old enough to be her father but he was rich and that seemed all Frederic cared about. Evelyn's venom rose anew "Frederic left me hardly any time to dress for dinner. I am afraid half this bath will be wasted, Bess."

Evelyn rose with reluctance from the warm tub. She stood in front of the fire to dress, for the evening's storms had cooled the air to an uncomfortable chill and gooseflesh prickled her limbs. Far too soon she was fit to descend.

8

The table had been set for an elaborate meal, with candles and fine china that had not been used since her father had entertained. A fire had been coaxed to great heights within the fireplace and the curtains were closed, hiding the sight of the storm if not the noise. Rain battered at the windows in a wash of sound.

Frederic had, to Evelyn's amazement, bathed and dressed and even combed his hair back into a neat style. She had almost forgotten her brother was a handsome man; how like their father he looked. It filled her with an unusual affection for him.

"Evening, Evelyn," he said as he took his seat and waved away the offer of a drink stronger than watered wine.

Evelyn looked at him, suspicious. Bathed and not drinking? He must want something from her. There was no other reason she could imagine for his behavior.

Choosing soberness and her company over an evening of anything else was so far from his usual behavior that he must want something very dear indeed. She would play the part until she found out the reason behind his antics, at least.

"Good evening, Frederic."

"How was your ride?"

"It was splendid. Diadem is coming along, and if she remains sound I hope to see her at the head of many hunts this autumn."

Frederic nodded along to her words. It resembled polite interest, even if it was feigned.

"Hunts here?" he asked. "At Evermont?"

"If the Duke agrees to it," said Evelyn, terse. "It is his stable, after all."

Frederic took a large swallow of wine. She watched the bob of his throat and noticed the beads of sweat on his forehead, as if he were under great strain. How much watered wine would it take for him to reach his usual state?

"Yes, about Pemberton..." He dabbed at his brow with his napkin. Evelyn's eyebrows rose. Did her brother know about the Duke's embrace? She fidgeted, trying to come up with some excuse for her behavior.

"We have been exchanging letters since his departure." Frederic trailed off, looking into his glass of wine. He set it aside with force, then picked up his fork and pushed the food around on his plate.

"Yes?" Evelyn prompted. The longer he delayed the more anxious she grew.

"Right," he began again, with a deep breath. "I would

like to host a gathering or two here at Evermont, to break up the monotony you know. I do miss London. Something small."

"Like a hunt?"

"A dinner was more what I was thinking," Frederic said.

Of course, Frederic did not ride.

"You did say a gathering or two. We could do both!" Evelyn could not hide her excitement.

She was so relieved that her brother had not mentioned her transgression with the Duke. He had probably not mentioned it to Frederic at all. "Please, Frederic. You do not need to ride in it."

Lightning illuminated the curtains and the trailing thunder shook Evelyn's bones.

"It must be just overhead," Frederic said, looking up at the painted ceiling. He got up from the table to peer out the window.

"I hope the horses are not frightened," Evelyn said, from her seat.

When he pulled back the curtain the rain grew louder, as if the fabric had been all that buffered them from the storm. Water ran in streams across the grass, forming puddles in the depressions and creating ruts in the paths, shaping the landscape to suit itself.

There was something of the storm's ferocity behind Frederic's eyes when he turned from the window. It was so unlike the dispirited Frederic she had grown used to. In the next flicker of lightning, it was gone. He looked fatigued as he slumped back into his chair.

"When I next write to Pemberton I will ask what he

thinks of the idea. He would enjoy it, the fool." Frederic spun the stem of his wineglass around in his fingers. "Lord Ashwood will be invited of course."

"Does the Duke know?" Evelyn asked at once, before she could stop herself.

Frederic frowned, looking up from the glass. "Why would Pemberton care if I invite the old man? As long as there are fresh-faced debutantes attending, he will be satisfied with the guest list."

Evelyn's ears burned. She sawed into the roasted mutton and shoved too large a bite into her mouth. Chewing gave her something to do other than incriminating herself.

"What is going on with you?" Frederic asked. He was far too astute when sober. "You look crazed. Please do not behave this way at the dinner. Have you forgotten how to eat?"

"I am feeling ill," she lied. "Excuse me. I will lie down for a moment and I am certain it will pass."

"Just a moment," he said, holding up a hand to stop her.

She sat back down and clenched her hands in her lap.

"I have invited Adele, from London. She will stay here as a guest for a time." His mouth tightened to a severe line.

"You did not!"

Frederic's wordless glare was enough to assure her that he had, and that he would hear no argument against it.

"Frederic, can you imagine what people will say! She

is a..." Evelyn glanced at her brother's face and changed her wording. "An actress. It just is not done."

"Nonsense," said Frederic. "She is often invited to London gatherings."

"The eccentrics of London may get away with that sort of behavior, Frederic, but they are not us." Evelyn could not believe her brother would go so far with this foolishness. She knew he was infatuated, but to bring her home to Evermont was to declare an entirely new level of intention. "There can be nothing between you two, nothing of substance, for she is not a woman of substance!"

Her brother clenched his hands around his wineglass until his knuckles were white. She wished that the Duke were here.

"I am not asking permission, Evelyn," Frederic said, between gritted teeth. "I am The Lord here."

"I am not questioning your right to make a thoughtless decision, Frederic; I am questioning the sense of it!" Evelyn folded her napkin into a neat square and slapped it down on the table.

"An actress as a guest here while Lord Ashwood visits? It will be a disaster!"

Though Frederic's face had gone the shade of purple that warned of an imminent outburst, the expected rage did not come. Instead, he took a deep breath and stared into the fire, its sizzling pops were interspersed between the growls of thunder. He did not speak again until the footmen had finishing serving the next course. Evelyn straightened the edge of the tablecloth.

"Adele will be our guest, and you will treat her kindly.

I will not have her humiliated." He took a breath and his face softened. He looked so like father when his eyes were kind. "Will you do that for me, Evelyn?" he asked softly.

If her brother did not look so desperate, she might have said no. Even as she nodded, her stomach was sinking. Something, she knew, was going to go terribly wrong.

"I will treat her as graciously as any guest at Evermont," Evelyn said. "Do not worry, brother."

She did not ask what he thought the other ladies attending would say of her. That was not her concern.

"Thank you," he said evenly. "Then I shall send a letter to Pemberton in the morning to ask about the hunt. I expect you will want to handle planning the dinner."

It was not a question.

"Yes, brother." Evelyn's reply was wooden.

It went unspoken that she would not be enjoying a hunt if she did not agree to treat her brother's actress as if she were a lady.

She retired to her bedroom, exhausted.

"Was it a pleasant dinner, my Lady?" Bess asked. She tugged the laces of Evelyn's corset free. "You look... well, drained."

"He is going to bring his actress to Evermont," Evelyn said, pulling her nightclothes down over her head. "Do you think he expects me to provide her with a wardrobe as well? I am sure her dresses will not be at all appropriate for polite company."

"If he has spent as much money on her as you have said he has, I am sure she will have dresses of her own to wear."

Bess made a good point. Evelyn sat down on the edge of the bed and drew her knees up beneath her chin.

"And Lord Ashwood will be here," Evelyn said.

That statement made the old maid's eyebrows shoot up.

"What about the Duke?"

Evelyn shook her head. "Frederic does not know about that, and really, what is there to tell? This dinner is going to be a disaster, Bess."

"You will manage, dear," Bess said, clucking her tongue. "You always do. Brilliant girl."

Evelyn looked miserably up at her maid from her seated position. Bess sighed.

"At least it shall not be boring, hmm?"

"At least." Evelyn replied.

She flipped on to her stomach and pulled the pillow over her head, drowning out the rain and thoughts of impending doom.

Her brother was an idiot, the Duke was far away, and Evelyn was coming unraveled.

9

The Duke of Pemberton replied to Frederic's letter in person. He rode in with a small retinue of servants on a Saturday morning while a fine drizzle of rain misted his clothes. Evelyn watched from the window. Her brother greeted him at the door and the two clasped hands with smiles on their faces.

She watched their lips move and wished she could read the conversation between them. Did The Duke ask after her? It had been six days since her talk with Frederic at dinner and Evelyn's nerves had been raw ever since.

Bess had pulled Evelyn's dresses from storage. Together, they were going through the garments and discarding those that had fallen out of fashion during the past year. Evelyn would have loved to go into town and order a new collection for the upcoming events, but their current finances would not allow such things.

She would make do with what she had. The debutantes Frederic had promised the Duke would be sure to have the latest dresses. Evelyn felt like a dowdy old women with last year's fashions. Pemberton would not even notice her. She needed to put this thought out of her mind.

"Are you going to go down and greet him?" Bess asked, brushing at a worn patch of fabric on a cerulean dress. "You are practically climbing through the window to get a look at him."

"Bess!" Evelyn said, aghast. "No. I will see them both at dinner."

"Oh, your blush, my Lady" Bess said with a smile.

Evelyn's face burned. Bess had been with the family so long, it made her entirely too free with her thoughts.

The men disappeared inside. Evelyn felt the front door close behind them, the thump rocking the old manor house. She stepped away from the window. Rain and grey sky had obscured her view, but she could have traced every line of the Duke with her eyes closed. The view inside was not half as nice to look at. Her bedroom was a mess of dresses and boxes and shoes.

"You look at a mess like a boy looks at green vegetables on his plate," Bess teased. "I will have it tidied up in a flash my Lady, do not worry yourself."

"I was only thinking that I should sell some," said Evelyn. "Then I could buy a more fashionable dress."

"Do you think the Duke will not like you well enough in one of these?" Bess asked, hands on her hips.

"Lord Ashwood, you mean," Evelyn said.

Bess huffed. "When you are married you will have the means to purchase any dress you choose. No need to sell these off."

The Duke's Wicked Wager

Married.

The word turned Evelyn equal parts excited and fearful. She had known the sort of marriage she would have had with her late fiancé: a companion throughout life. Their relationship was an easy camaraderie; predictable. She could imagine the marriage she would have with the aging Lord Ashwood, if her brother had his way. Brief, uneasy, and dutiful.

What would a marriage to the Duke be like? Challenging, frustrating, breathtaking. Yes, she could picture it. Evelyn had nothing to offer but herself and he had his choice of young debutantes. She was being ridiculous. She had to put him out of her mind. The sound of his laughter carried up the stairs, rolling through her like a warm stream.

"Bess?" Evelyn asked, voice small.

The old woman poked her head in from the side room, where Evelyn's clothes were kept.

"I have changed my mind," Evelyn said. "I will go down now. Please help me dress."

"Right away, my Lady."

THE MEN WERE PLAYING at billiards in the gaming parlor. This was one game where Frederic could best the Duke, for the latter lacked the ability to predict the trajectory of the balls before they were hit. The green covered table was one of the last things her father had purchased before his death and it was a prized possession, a rarity even in the wealthier homes. He had taught both of his children the rules of the game and they had taken to it with gusto.

"Ah, Lady Evelyn," the Duke said, turning at the sound of her slippered footsteps with the billiard cue in his hand. "Care for a game?"

She glanced at Frederic. Her brother looked sober, but miserable. His face was contorted in an uncomfortable grimace and a sheen of sweat glistened on his forehead. He had seemed ill of late.

"Your Grace, are you attempting to weasel out of a losing game?" she taunted. "I shall play the winner."

The Duke's smile was open and easy, unlike her own tremulous attempt at it. She was torn in her emotions, wanting at once to embrace him and to hide from him.

"Then you will be facing your brother, I am ashamed to say." Pemberton bent back over the table and surveyed his situation. "I should have stuck with cards."

"He is dreadful, Evelyn," Frederic said, with a rare gleeful grin. "Really quite embarrassing in a man of your quality."

"Bah," the Duke waved an unconcerned hand. "Coming from the man who will ride naught but an ancient pony. What will you do when that poor Peanut dies?"

"That is not the same thing at all!" Frederic protested. "And her name is Peacock."

He almost seemed her brother of old. Together they both seemed better version of themselves, the Duke less self-important and Frederic... well, sober. Evelyn tucked herself onto the sofa beneath a window, a comfortable cushion laid out with pillows. The dark wallpaper and the mahogany floors gave the gaming parlor a masculine feel, but the sofa was distinctly feminine with its floral brocade and velveteen pillows. Frederic had not been jesting at Pemberton's expense; the Duke was truly wretched at billiards. When the ball ricocheted away from his intended net for the fourth time, Evelyn took pity on him.

"May I offer a few suggestions?" Evelyn asked. She stood and brushed her skirts down over her thighs. "I see my brother is in no hurry to improve upon your playing."

Frederic rested his stick on the ground and leaned his weight on it. "Oh come now, let me have something! Is it not enough that he bests me at lawn games, cards, and chess?"

"It is too pitiful, Frederic, have a heart!"

"With some instruction I could perhaps manage to prolong the suffering of all players," the Duke said good-naturedly.

"We will have to hide the table when our guests arrive," said Evelyn, tugging the cue from Pemberton's hands. "Or your billiards' catastrophes will be the talk of London!"

The Duke covered his face in mock shame. "I will never be able to face Society again! Oh, the gentleman's plight!"

Evelyn held the cue between her fingers and demonstrated a hit. The ball rolled with vigor into the pocket. Pemberton applauded.

"You hit too hard," Evelyn said, handing it back to the Duke. His fingers brushed hers as he took it, and the look he gave her said it was intentional. For just a moment she couldn't breathe. Then she caught her thought. "There is more to it than force, Your Grace. Finesse is required, and a sense of timing."

"Next you will tell me I ought to keep my eyes open when I hit," he said. "I cannot just aim the stick at the place I wish it to go and hope for the best."

"Probably not," she said with a laugh.

"Should I keep my eyes open as well?"

"That would be a start."

The Duke attempted another shot. It went as haphazard as ever, but this time did not ricochet off the walls of the table and threaten to leap across the room. It rolled to a limp stop a foot from the net.

"Well, that is an improvement." He handed the cue back to Evelyn and took her seat beneath the window. "Show me how it is done. A little brother and sister rivalry."

Frederic cocked his head at Evelyn. She considered him a moment, his face red and sweating; then nodded. They played until the servants came in to light the lanterns, as darkness had crept in without their notice. Both Everings had won their share of games.

"And that is six for the fairer sex," said the Duke. He clapped his hands and stood. "And four for poor Lord Evermont, bested by his sister."

"You have no room to brag," Evelyn chided. "You were too frightened to face me at all!"

"And that decision proved to be one of my best," the Duke said. "No, I shall keep my dignity intact for another day at least, thank you."

Frederic's mood had turned dour as the evening

progressed. He had loosened his cravat and unbuttoned the top button of his shirt, but still beads of sweat collected at his temples and in his hair. Pemberton clasped Frederic's shoulder and took him aside. Despite the rain's increasing volume, Evelyn could just hear them.

"Are you well, Frederic?" the Duke asked, his wide brow creased with concern. He glanced over his shoulder. Evelyn turned away in a hurry, attempting to look busy. "You look ill. Should we cancel our plans? I do not wish to overburden you, if you are unwell."

Evelyn tidied the gaming parlor. She could have gone ahead to the dining room, but her curiosity was peaked. If her brother had felt ill, why had he not called for the doctor, nor told his friend of it before the man came to visit?

"If I could just have a drink stronger than watered down swill at dinner, I would be fine." Frederic spat the words. "My mood is erratic. I feel joyous, then low, then furious, with no more reason for one emotion than the next. I feel mad, George."

"You are not mad," said the Duke. "It will pass. It is a drinking sickness, I have seen another man go through much the same thing, but far worse. His was from opium."

"I cannot keep food down." Frederic pressed the palm of his hand to his forehead. "I do not want Adele to see me like this. We should call this whole thing off."

Evelyn agreed. Though, if the woman saw Frederic in such a state perhaps she would be frightened off once and for all. She rolled the three billiard balls into a row against the low rail. The red ball bore a dent from the

Duke's efforts to learn the game. Thumbing the battle scar, Evelyn listened with bated breath for the Duke's reply.

He sighed first. "We cannot, my friend. The invitations have been sent and it took all of my weight to persuade anyone respectable to attend. If you squander this chance, I do not know if there is anything I can do to help you. Evelyn will be doomed to spinsterhood."

"Blast it all," Frederic said. "I knew you would say it, but still. Blast."

"We will manage."

"I pray for a shred of your confidence, Pemberton."

Frederic turned and stopped as if surprised to see Evelyn still present. There was a unique ability, Evelyn thought, among brothers to forget entirely the existence of their sisters.

"It was a mess in here," Evelyn said. "You were not going to tidy it up."

"Heaven help any man who marries you, Evelyn," said Frederic. "One thing out of place and I swear, you flitter about it. It will drive a man mad."

Frederic and the Duke headed toward the dining room and she followed. The Duke was dressed in fine, expensive clothes. He wore them in his intentional, mussed way. If Evelyn had to bet, she would put money on him spending just as much time creating his disheveled look as most men did crafting a perfect one. Vain man. She wondered if he did that just to bother her, knowing she wanted nothing more than to straighten his cravat, even out the collar, and smooth his rumpled shirt. Of course she would never do that. She would tell him…

Oh bother. She felt a blush climbing up her neck at her thoughts, and then he was at her shoulder.

"Your brother tells me you would like to a host a hunt, Lady Evelyn," the Duke said, taking a sip of the watered wine her brother had called swill. He curled his lip in distaste and Frederic gave him a look that said, 'you see?'

Evelyn sat up a bit straighter. "Yes, I would, Your Grace, if you please. I have been training Diadem for hunting and it would be a perfect test for her. Just a lawn meet to being the season, if a willing hunt master can be found."

"Diadem? That is the mare from the match race, is it not?" The Duke asked. "It will be easy enough to find a hunt master looking to train his young hounds before the season truly begins."

"It is, yes." She frowned. "She will not race again. She cannot stay sound under intense training."

"That's a shame. She is beautiful. But she has taken to hunting?"

"Very much so!" Evelyn said, nodding. "She has a natural talent for it, but I have yet to see how she will handle herself with the hunting crowd. It is a different thing entirely to have other horses running beside you and hounds baying at your feet. She may lose her head."

"With you as her rider? I doubt that. Well, it sounds as though you have your hopes pinned on this hunt," said the Duke. "I would hate to disappoint you."

Frederic snorted dismissively at their conversation. "Lovely. Horses."

10

The guests began to arrive the following week. The Duke had brought an army of servants with him, enough to bolster the ranks of Evermont's skeleton staff into a respectable showing. Together, the servants new and old had opened the disused sections of the manor. It had taken the entire week to set the guest rooms to rights, removing the white sheets that protected the furniture, throwing open the windows to let in fresh air, and dusting the cobwebs from the ceilings. The floors gleamed and the furniture smelled of polish. The hum of activity recalled Evelyn to her childhood. Her mother had been an eager and attentive hostess before her illness, and her father had been an indulgent and gracious host until her death. After that, the Evermont manor had been a family only affair.

Now, it buzzed like a hive in springtime. Though the sky was a constant and even shade of grey, the house was lit with fireplaces and lanterns, all casting a warm glow. The kitchens worked with fervor and the smells of bread and stew scented the air, masking the scent of old cigar smoke and dust. Evelyn, Frederic, and the Duke waited in the entry hall, dressed in their finest. Pemberton was a perfect gentleman. He knew every guest's name and greeted them as old friends, with a familiar handshake and an inquiry after their families or their health.

Only three days. She only had to play the hostess for three days; a day for the guests to settle, the day of the lawn meet, and the day of departure. Still, much could go wrong in so short a time.

"Good evening, Lord Ashwood," said the Duke.

Evelyn snapped her attention to the present. The Duke shook the hand of a man much plumper, shorter, and older than he. Frederic introduced the man to Evelyn. Lord Ashwood's greeting was far too exuberant to sit comfortably with Evelyn, and she wondered how far Frederic had assured him of their eventual betrothal. She shot her brother a glare. It went ignored, however, for the next person to walk in the door was a woman of uncommon beauty.

Her hair was strawberry blonde with just a touch of red and her eyes were a deep, chocolate shade of brown. The cut of her dress was the height of fashion and impeccably tailored, displaying her figure to great advantage. All of the eyes were on her, men and women alike. Evelyn prayed this was not one of the debutantes her brother had arranged to entertain the Duke. She could never compete with this.

"Miss Adele Bouchard," Pemberton announced as the woman batted her fan in a coquettish flourish.

Frederic had gone red, his usual shade of late. His mouth opened and closed. Evelyn took pity on him.

"How wonderful to meet you at last, Miss Bouchard," Evelyn said, striding over to the woman and taking her by the arm. "I have heard the most wonderful things about you."

"Please, call me Adele," the woman said. Her smile wide and guileless, showing even white teeth and cupid bow lips. "You must be my dear Frederic's sweet sister, Lady Evelyn."

"Did Frederic call me sweet?" Evelyn asked. "He must have been in a rare mood."

Frederic at last managed to produce words, threatened by the thought of Evelyn steering the conversation. He hurried up beside them as Evelyn led Adele, the last of the guests, from the room.

"Miss Bouchard!" he barked. It was too loud by half and the woman winced. He tried again. "Please, Adele, may we speak before you go to your rooms?"

She frowned, and Evelyn thought she would refuse him, but she relented with a pert nod.

"I cannot wait to get to know you, Evelyn," said Adele, seizing Evelyn by the arms and kissing her cheeks in the manner of the French. "I hope we will be as dear as sisters!"

Frederic drew Adele to a private corner of the room. Evelyn fought the desire to eavesdrop, and was saved from temptation by the Duke's voice beside her ear.

"A moment alone at last," he said, in that low purr

that made her shiver, bone deep. "The guests have been seen to their rooms and we will have some time before they are recovered from their travels. Five in all, though I expect ten more for the lawn meet, to ride in tomorrow."

Evelyn gestured to where Frederic and Adele were cloistered beside a bronze statue. Their conversation had grown heated judging by the flurry of gesticulations from Adele. Frederic's voice rose in booms; then dropped to a whisper.

"She is beautiful," she said. "I can see now why Frederic is besotted with her beyond all semblances of good sense and reason."

"An exceptional beauty," the Duke agreed, annoyingly. "She is, to my surprise, as besotted with him as he is with her."

"She does not seem to feel kindly toward him at the moment."

The woman's French accent had grown thicker, thick enough that Evelyn could not have discerned the words even if she *had* been eavesdropping. Which she was not.

"They had a row of sorts, before Frederic left London." The Duke shook his head before she could ask. "I do not know what it was over, and Frederic would not tell me. It has been tearing him apart. He only left the city because she demanded he do so."

"I hope they do not argue the whole visit," said Evelyn, fretting. "That will ruin things."

"All will be well, Lady Evelyn. Do not worry." He placed his hand at the small of her back, a familiar, intimate gesture that brought heat to her skin. Evelyn sidestepped out of his reach.

"Your Grace," she began.

"You do not wish to marry Lord Ashwood," he said, over her protests. He cupped her cheek and she leaned into the touch, unable to stop herself from the show of weakness.

"I do not know him. He may be the best husband a woman could hope for."

"Nonsense. He is not the sort of man a woman like you should be with," the Duke said, dismissing the man with a wave of his hand.

"And who should I be with, Your Grace?" Evelyn pushed his hand away from her with sudden vehemence. How dare he presume to give her orders? He was not her father, nor her brother. "To you, this may be a game. To me, it is my entire future. Please, Excuse me."

IT WAS easy enough to avoid the Duke. With the house full to bursting with guests and staff, there was always someone to spend time with, and if that failed, she hid in the stable. She could not decide if she was hiding from him out of anger or out of fear she would not be able to keep her wits around him, but the result was the same. On occasion she had seen him passing down a hall and watched him, unseen, with a painful sort of longing in her chest.

Frederic was pleased at her attention to Lord Ashwood, something she threw herself into mostly to irritate the Duke. She had sat with Lord Ashwood for tea. They had played a game of chess. She had listened to him read aloud from his favorite books. He was a polite old man and the epitome of a gentleman. The conversation never grew stale. Once, she would have been content with a marriage of friendship, but having glimpsed something of the realm of passion she now longed for that spark. That dangerous thrill she felt when the Duke touched her, or caught her eye across the room.

She was immersed in a game of whist, with Lord Ashwood as her partner and Frederic and Lady Comerford as their opponents. Dinner had been a success, to Evelyn's surprise. The unusual assortment of guests managed small talk and Adele had been charming and refined.

"I think we have this one," Lady Comerford said to Frederic.

Frederic raised dubious eyebrows. They were behind by two points, and Evelyn's team had only one to go. Evelyn tapped her finger on the back of her hand of cards, signaling to Lord Ashwood. He played his trump card.

"That is seven," Lord Ashwood said. Evelyn cheered.

Frederic tossed his cards down with a groan. "That is it for me. I cannot lose another round."

"Oh you spoilsport," Lady Comerford groused.

Lord Ashwood then proposed a game of billiards, which Frederic agreed to. He would never refuse a game he could win. Lady Comerford opted to watch, while Evelyn excused herself under the pretense of visiting the kitchens. It was there she ran into the Duke at last.

She spotted a familiar tousled pile of hair and a rumpled coat from the back, but he was not alone.

The Duke's Wicked Wager

Evelyn's stomach churned with acid. Never had jealousy struck her with such force. Turning from the scene with a gasp, she fled. Was it a servant girl? Tears dripped down her nose before she realized she was crying. Her vision fogged from tears and she did not notice the person until she smacked into them with a heavy thud.

"*Mon dieu!*"

"I am s-so sorry," Evelyn gasped out between hyperventilation. "Did I hurt you? I was not paying attention."

Adele rubbed at the red bruise forming on her forehead in the shape of Evelyn's shoulder.

"It will be fine," she said. "But what is this? What has upset you so?"

The petite Frenchwoman took Evelyn in hand and drew her into the sitting room. She rang for a servant and ordered a tray of tea with a touch of brandy, as comfortably as if she lived there. Then she sat beside Evelyn on the chaise and pulled her into a hug until Evelyn stopped crying. With a flourish, Adele presented Evelyn with a lacy handkerchief and a cup of the spiked tea. She took both gratefully.

"It is nothing," Evelyn said, when she could breathe again. She could not divulge her secrets, and the Duke's, to a total stranger.

Adele snorted. It was inelegant and unladylike and warmed Evelyn toward the woman immediately. "I am an actress, *ma chére*. You cannot lie to me, for I do it with more skill."

She tipped a bit more brandy into Evelyn's teacup. It smelled more of brandy than tea now.

"Tell me," Adele insisted.

Evelyn did. She held nothing back, telling the woman everything starting with her fiancé's death to her stolen and illicit embrace with the Duke. It was cathartic, but once it was spilled out she realized she could not take it back. She looked up to see the woman's reaction. Adele took a sip straight from the brandy bottle. Then she set it down on the tray, crossed her hands in her lap, and looked at Evelyn.

"You have been through too much to be putting your heart in the hands of a man like the Duke of Pemberton." Evelyn bristled. "No, do not argue."

She shut her mouth.

"He is a kind and amusing man, but he is not ready for marriage my Lady," said Adele. "Do not give your heart to a man who has no idea what to do with it once it is his."

Her words were far too close to the truth Evelyn's soul already knew. It was time to set aside the Duke and save herself any more heartache. At least she had found a friend in Adele.

THAT EVENING, the Duke found her. After her tea with Adele, Evelyn walked to the stables, ostensibly to check on Diadem before the lawn meet in the morning. Being close to the warm live creatures settled her and the scents of the clean stable were a comfort.

"Beautiful girl."

Evelyn's heart gave a traitorous thump when she

heard his voice in the aisle. Did it not know how awful this man was for it? Foolish heart. There was nowhere to hide unless she fled for Stanton's office and barricaded herself inside. Diadem snuffed a nervous breath through her nostrils as if she picked up on Evelyn's anxiety.

The Duke turned following the attention of the horse. "Lady Evelyn," he said. He was far too handsome as always.

"Your Grace," Evelyn replied.

There was no one else in the aisle. Not a groom to save her.

"You have been avoiding me." The Duke tapped his fingers along the top of Diadem's stall door, and Diadem coaxed him for treats. Had he been feeding her?

"I have seen less of you now that I am a guest at your house than when I visit. It is most unfair."

"I am not avoiding you," Evelyn lied. If he could pretend to care for her, she could pretend not to care for him. "I have been busy. As the hostess, I have many guests to attend to."

"Do you remember when I recommend that you never play at cards? Your bluffing face has not improved in the least since then. You are lying to me."

"And what if I am?" Evelyn said. "I cannot be seen having private encounters with you while I am hoping to find a husband. You will mark me spoiled."

"You are too concerned over your reputation," the Duke said.

Evelyn narrowed her eyes at him. "It is a simple thing for you to say, Your Grace. You are a man and a Duke besides; your reputation is a less fragile thing than mine. If you cared for me at all, you would leave me be."

The Duke's face tightened with traces of pain. She hoped, for a fleeting moment, he would announce his intention toward her. When he did not, she pushed past him and fled the stables. Evelyn was tired of running from the man.

11

*E*velyn woke before the sun. She hoped to be down for breakfast before even the Duke was awake, and at the stable with time to spare. Her riding habit, a sturdy teal affair, was tied up for walking. The house was still abed. Only servants moved with quiet footsteps and hushed words, lighting the fires and preparing for the day to come. She slipped past them down the stairs and into the breakfast parlor, where Bess had seen her coffee was ready. The strong bitter drink was just the thing before a hunt.

The dining room was empty. The curtains had not yet been pulled back but a fire was stirring in the hearth, beginning to creep up the logs with hungry licks of flame. She could not eat, for food never settled in her stomach on hunt days. Just as she drained the last of her coffee, the Duke entered. Evelyn's fingers shook as she set the cup down onto its saucer.

"Lady Evelyn," he said, but she was already standing and pushing past him through the door.

He did not stop her. Stanton and the groom staff had likely been up for hours yet and they would not be surprised to see her there. Anticipation had spread to the horses. They passed shrill whinnies to each other and tossed their heads as they were lead from their stalls to be groomed. She let the excitement in the stables wash away the terrible knot of tension that had seized her stomach at the sight of the Duke this morning. The man caused nothing but trouble, just with his presence.

She passed the next hour getting underfoot in the stable. Twice a groom had to coax a horse by her, so lost in thought was she that she stood in the middle of the aisle with her mind elsewhere. On the Duke, of course. Would he not put her out of her misery yet? If he could just tell her one way or the other if he had any intention toward her beyond a quick dalliance, she could act. It was the not knowing that killed her. If he had put her aside she could move on and give Lord Ashwood a fair chance. Marrying him would not be so awful, she thought, if only she did not still have her heart lent out to the Duke. Evelyn leaned against a stall door and sighed. The horse, curious about its new neighbor, rested its head on her shoulder and nibbled at her collar.

It was not one of hers. She shied away realizing that it may be a mouthy stallion. The thick necked creature must be one of her guest's and looked a proper hunting horse, all old-blooded bulk.

"That is the Duke's horse," Stanton said.

Evelyn bolted away from the door. The stable master laughed and she rubbed a self-conscious hand over her neck.

"Well I do not think it is contagious," he said. "He is not so hot tempered as the Duke's other horses. Still, he's a proud one with more muscle than sense."

"All looks and no substance, like the Duke himself."

Stanton only raised his eyebrows at that. Of course, the Duke was his new employer.

"Not long before the hunt now," said Stanton changing the subject. "Will you be wanting to see to Diadem, my Lady?"

She nodded. "Her first test! I do not expect us to be in the front of the field, with the old-hats here to show off, but I do hope we will keep up and not be left hill-topping."

"She is too quick for that. No, she may lose some time over the obstacles, or fussing about the noise, but I bet she will make it up through the fields and the flat of the paths."

"Of course we are not out there to show off. It is a training exercise and nothing more."

"But if the Duke happened to finish well behind you," Stanton said with a knowing smirk, "it would not be such an awful thing, hmm?"

"You are far too astute, Stanton. No, it would not be an awful thing at all." She flashed an impish grin. "I was a fool to lose my head over the man." As if it were not still lost.

Riders had begun to file into the stables. The women

were dressed in shades of blue and green, a light pallet to lend brightness to the grey fall day. Men walked in groups of twos and threes, placing bets on the outcome of the day. She did not see Frederic in the crowd. Maybe he had decided against taking part after all. Evelyn scuffed her boots on the stones and waited for a groom to bring Diadem to her. Amid the crowd of natural colors, a spot of vibrant red and brown demanded attention. Adele.

The woman caught sight of Evelyn at the same moment and let out a delighted squeal, all five feet of her frame colliding with Evelyn in a violent sort of hug. Breathless, she stepped back.

"It is too early, Evie!" Adele said, crinkling her nose in distaste. "Why must we be awake and about at such a hateful hour?"

Despite the woman's claims, she looked well-rested and lovely as ever.

"Do you ride, Adele?" Evelyn asked, curious. She had never known an actress, and wondered if they kept a horse.

"Some, yes," she said. "Frederic said there would be a horse for me, though I do not see him here."

She looked around, standing on tiptoes to see over the hats and horses.

"I would be surprised if he was," said Evelyn, looking around as well. "He is terrified of horses."

"Is he?" asked Adele. She looked amused. "Oh I must tease him about that."

They were interrupted by the arrival of Diadem. She looked full of herself and splendid in the polished tack, graceful neck arching as she danced over the ground. Evelyn took the reins from the groom.

"Please saddle Ella for Lady Adele," Evelyn said to the groom, who dipped his head and scurried off.

She waited for Adele's horse to arrive before mounting Diadem. Ella was a sweet old thing, placid but not slow. The mare would take a command if the rider knew how to ask for it, and would be content to follow otherwise. If Frederic were attending, he might have ridden her, but she still did not see him. Riders gathered at the edge of the stable yard where the hunt master towered above on a monstrous chestnut. Somewhere nearby, the hound master had the dogs ready to go. She could hear their yelping barks rising in intensity.

The groom returned several moments later with a fully saddled Ella. He held the mare's head while another of his fellows assisted Evelyn and then Adele onto their mounts.

"Well, I do not think I will be keeping up with you for long," Adele said, bringing Bella alongside Diadem.

"Ah, there is Frederic," Evelyn said, catching sight of her brother at last. She waved to him and he waved back, with a smile she thought was more for Adele than herself.

He was not pink and sweating for once. Perhaps the sickness had at last run its course. Evelyn glanced at Adele. The woman's smile at the sight of her brother was so sincere; it could not be for show. No, the woman, for better or worse, did seem to care for her brother. Lord help her.

"Sister," Frederic said, with a small bow for her and

Adele. "Miss Bouchard." His smile was a private thing for Adele alone. They shared an intimate look in which a thousand things were spoken without words. Evelyn blushed and looked away.

If she had doubted her brother's feelings for the actress were anything more than infatuation, the last tendrils of skepticism were being swept away.

"Will you ride, Frederic?" Evelyn asked.

He was dressed to, but he paled at her words.

"Oh please, Frederic!" Adele cheered. "Ride alongside me. I will be left in your sister's dust the moment the horn is blown and I do not wish to be alone in the woods."

Frederic puffed up his chest. "How can I refuse?"

Her brother flagged a groom down from across the yard and the man came running. Frederic hesitated so Evelyn chimed in. She could not truly leave her brother with old Peacock.

"Perhaps Duchess? If she is not claimed," Evelyn said.

The groom chewed his lip. "I think she is not, Lady Evelyn. I shall return in a moment."

Frederic gave her a grateful look. In a moment of braveness he laid his hand on Ella's neck. Some of the effect was lost when he flinched away from the questioning snuffle of the mare's nose. Diadem jigged beneath Evelyn, feeding off her rider's impatience. She let the mare have her head, putting some space between herself and the lovebirds. Then, she saw the Duke. He was leading the thick-bodied warmblood from the stable, looking as regal as his mount. The two were a fine pair. Full of themselves and with much reason to be. Diadem could have thrown her then and she would not have noticed, so fixed were her eyes on the man. As if he felt them, he looked up. Beneath the brim of his hat, his eyes met hers.

His expression was unguarded, and the twist of pain behind it sent an ache to her heart. In a flash, that was gone, and his jovial look was back. He tipped his hat at her and swung into the saddle. The Duke pressed his heels against the horse's flanks and guided it through the crowd, straight toward her with the unwavering intensity of a fish swimming upstream. Before he reached her, a horse bumped into Diadem.

"Whoa!" Lord Ashwood blushed and tugged on his horse's reins. The mare tossed her head and skittered sideways. "Good morning, Lady Evelyn. Eager to be off?"

"Good morning, Lord Ashwood," Evelyn replied. When she looked up again, the Duke was in conversation with Adele and Frederic, who had mounted Duchess. Had the Duke been coming towards her at all?

Lord Ashwood was still speaking. She forced her attention back to the man. In his youth, he might have been attractive, but age had drawn him down in, soft flesh and he had indulged too much in food and drink for what had been muscle on a younger man had turned to a bulge around his middle. There was nothing about him that ignited passion within her. But he was safe. A sensible choice. Evelyn was always sensible; at least, she had been.

"Oh, it looks as if we are about to begin," Evelyn said, pointing to where the hound and hunt masters had come together. A trumpet blast called for the horses to gather.

Lord Ashwood and Evelyn clucked their horses over to the group. It was chaos; dogs barking and horses dancing eager to be off. Breath billowed, and turned to fog in the crisp fall air. Evelyn breathed it in, loving every moment of it as she circled Diadem to steady her. Another blast of the trumpet and the hunt master was off, into the hills. The group followed at their leisure; until the fox was spotted there was no need for speed. She stayed close to Lord Ashwood. He was a capable and confident rider.

The Duke of Pemberton was ahead, riding with a woman she did not know. Was it the one from the kitchens? Frederic and Adele had already fallen to the back of the pack where they could ride at whatever pace suited them. Evelyn hoped Frederic would not embarrass himself by falling off.

"I am so enjoying this visit to Evermont," Lord Ashwood nearly yelled over the cacophony. "I do hope you will be a guest at my home, with your brother of course. In the wintertime, perhaps?"

"Do you keep a stable, Lord Ashwood?" she asked. Diadem was acting up, shaking her head in defiance and half-rearing. She wanted to be moving. "Easy, girl. Easy."

"I do, I do," said Lord Ashwood. "Though it is not half as impressive as Evermont's, I am afraid. Your brother tells me you are a master horsewoman and are responsible entirely for the success. During your time at my estate you might lend me some of that expertise."

Evelyn's heart did leap at that. She could scarcely believe that Frederic had spoken so well of her. Maybe he was just eager to be rid of her.

"I would enjoy that," she said, and realized it was the truth. It would not be so dreadful to marry this man. Diadem's danced again, hooves flashing.

"Lady Evelyn!" Lord Ashwood pulled his horse up.

Diadem dropped her front feet onto the ground with a thud. Evelyn circled the mare, giving her something to do with her mind other than work herself up.

"Please go on ahead. Diadem is fresh to the hunt and she only needs a bit of space to calm herself."

He nodded and kicked his horse up into the main pack. Evelyn, focused on working Diadem through bending exercises, did not notice the Duke's approach.

"She is a handful today," he said. He had reined his horse up a short distance away to watch. "Do you need to return to the stable?"

"No, she will settle," Evelyn said. "It is only all the noise getting to her. She hates to be still and wait."

"A horse after my own heart."

"Your riding companion will leave you behind if you dally, Your Grace," said Evelyn. At last Diadem settled with a huff.

The Duke shrugged. "I hardly know the woman. But what of Lord Ashwood?"

It did not seem so dangerous to speak on horseback. He could not touch her there. They brought their horses side by side at a trot and headed toward the group.

"We are not a match," she said, flippant. "On the field, I mean. His horse will lag before two miles have passed. Diadem will not."

"I have learned not to doubt you where horses are

concerned," he said. "Since we have, by chance, ended up here together we may as well ride as a pair."

Evelyn's fingers tightened on the reins. They should not. Out of the corner of her eye she could not help but admire the figure he cut in the saddle, straight-backed and proud, his hands easy on the reins. Before she could respond, three trumpet cries tore the air.

"They have it!" Evelyn gasped. She spurred Diadem to a canter and the Duke did the same beside her.

Over the hills they went. Horses began to flag and drop back from the pack, while Evelyn and the Duke moved up. Diadem, with the Duke's horse close beside her, seemed to think it a race and worked to keep up with the bigger horse, whose strides ate the ground in great leaps. When they moved from the field to the forest, it was five of them at the front of the pack and Evelyn had yet to ask Diadem for speed.

"She flies!" The Duke yelled. His face was split in a wide open grin, as boyish and uncynical as she had ever seen him. She knew that joy was reflected in her own eyes and they rushed to the hunt.

They crashed through the woods, hooves striking hard-packed dirt and crunching leaves. Evelyn leaned low over Diadem's neck to avoid the grasping branches. She leapt the first log on the ground, but the second was at an odd angle. Evelyn did not see it until it was too late to react. The Duke's horse leap the first and second in quick succession, the trained beast never hesitating, but Diadem skidded to a stop and Evelyn, unable to compensate, flew over the mare's head. The peculiar sensation of being airborne was halted in sudden, terrifying contact with the ground.

~~~

She woke. Concerned faces hovered above her,

"Lady Evelyn?" someone was saying her name, over and over. Someone else was shaking her. She lifted a hand to push them off. Her body was a mass of pain and something sharp and warm woke when she moved.

"Do not move," said a voice. It was commanding and it calmed her just to hear it. The Duke. "Stop shaking her you idiot."

"I beg your pardon?" another man's voice. Older. Lord Ashwood.

"It is not the time for wounded pride," the Duke said, and it was a snarl. "Move aside."

Lord Ashwood gasped. She imagined Pemberton had followed his request with a more physical command. Arms, solid and warm, wrapped around and lifted her from the ground. Blackness threatened at the edges of her vision.

"She is swooning again!" Adele's voice, sounding thin and far away. "Put her on Ella, her brother can take her home."

"I will ride with her," the Duke said. He left no room for arguments, but Evelyn could imagine the scandalized whispers of the riders around her. She tried to stir and push him away, but his arms were solid as stone.

They lurched and she felt movement beneath her, the Duke's horse. Lucky it was such a big beast now, carrying two all the way home. The roaring in her ears was growing louder, her vision tightened to pin pricks.

"Rest now, Evelyn," the Duke's voice was a whisper. "I have you."

She did not have much choice, for blackness claimed her.

Part 3

Promise Me This Dance

12

Lady Evelyn Evering woke alone. A pain blossomed in her head when she opened her eyes, and she shut them again. With a groan, she rubbed a hand over her face and along the back of her skull, searching for the source of her misery. She winced when her fingers found a lump. The skin was tender and warm with swelling, but she did not feel blood. Tentatively, she opened her eyes again. Her bedroom was bright with sunshine and she could hear the fire in the hearth, but did not dare turn to look at it.

She was in her bed with a pile of pillows beneath her head and blankets pulled up to her chin as if she were sick. It was unbearably warm. Evelyn groaned again. Alone in the room and unable to move, she had no choice but to lie in her bed and sweat through her nightclothes. Someone had changed her into them, for she could not remember going to bed the night before, nor what she had done to cause such a terrible wound. Her thoughts were a nebulous cloud and the more she chased after them, the farther away they drifted. Blindly reaching out, Evelyn fumbled for the bell pull beside her bed to summon a servant to aid her.

"Oh, Lady Evelyn!" Miss Adele Bouchard's gleeful exclamation was heartwarming, but painful. Evelyn flinched as the shrill sound sent a stab of pain through her head. "Oh dear, I am sorry. It is just, you have been asleep so long; we were beginning to fear you would not wake."

Adele sniffled. She came into Evelyn's view, looking weary and raw with her porcelain skin a blotchy shade of pink, as if this was not her first crying spell. The petite Frenchwoman sat down on the edge of Evelyn's bed and reached for Evelyn's hand.

"I should tell your brother that you are awake," said Adele, giving Evelyn's hand a soft squeeze. Her hand was as polished and delicate as the rest of her. "He has been worrying himself into such a state, and he takes it out with a temper. Half of the staff hide from him now."

It was just as well that Adele had taken control of the conversation because Evelyn was not certain she could speak. Her throat was dry, whether from disuse or the still air, and when she opened her mouth nothing came out.

"Oh do not try to speak yet." Adele's look changed from concerned friend to mother hen in a blink. "The doctor said that you should not attempt too much at once, if you woke. When you woke, I mean. I meant when you woke."

The Duke's Wicked Wager

Adele looked down at their linked hands. She took a deep breath to steady herself.

"The Duke of Pemberton returned home." Her tone was conciliatory, gentle. She did not meet Evelyn's eyes as she spoke. "But Lord Ashwood is still here. He sent for the finest doctor from London and insisted on paying for it all. It was the day after that the Duke left, and I have never seen someone so out of sorts."

Evelyn's mind struggled to follow the line of conversation. Words swam to the forefront as if more important than the others around them. The Duke, George Pender. Those words came with a familiar face. But he had gone; he had left Evermont without waiting to see if she would wake up. It did not seem the behavior of a man who cared at all.

"Do not cry, Evelyn, please," Adele begged. She reached up to smooth Evelyn's hair back from her face with tender fingers. "It was all such a mess when it happened. Emotions were high and I thought it might come to a duel between Lord Ashwood and the Duke. Pemberton left to ensure it would not happen, and he was correct to do so."

It was all too much to think about when she could scarce manage to think at all. Evelyn stroked her throat in a pleading gesture.

"*Mon dieu*! How unconscionable of me." Adele tugged the bell pull. "Of course you need the doctor straight away. I was being selfish, but I was just so relieved to see you wake!"

Adele brushed Evelyn's cheeks with two kisses and rose from the bed. She was out of Evelyn's view, but she heard the door to her bedroom open and hushed, excited voices from the other side. A moment later, a man came into sight with Adele at his side.

"Lady Evelyn, how happy we are to see you awake." The man, the doctor Evelyn assumed, bent over the bed. His fingers prodded and poked at her skull. "It is healing quite well. Head wounds bleed a shocking amount, but it is what is happening inside rather than outside that worried me."

Adele was frowning at the man with dislike. "Must you stab at her? Look at her, can you not see it pains her!"

The doctor and Adele surveyed each other with mutual expressions of annoyance. Evelyn was certain it was not the first time such a dispute had occurred over her.

"I am a doctor," the man said, drawing himself up. "Please sit down and allow me to work."

He pointed toward the corner of the room Evelyn could not see. Adele obliged, but with a fierce expression that left no doubt she would be watching the man from her seat. The doctor tutted. From the leather bag at his side he removed two bottles, cloudy glass obscuring their contents. Evelyn watched with interest as he poured a dab of the liquid into a vial and held it out to her.

"A sip of this and I think you will be feeling up to talking," he said, thrusting it at her again when she did not immediately take it.

Adele swept in and nudged the man out of the way with her hip, snatching the vial from him with a word of French that did not need an English translation for its meaning to be clear.

"Tilt your head back, *ma amie*," Adele coaxed. She lifted the vial to Evelyn's lips and tipped the liquid into her mouth. It tasted of cinnamon and cloves and burned Evelyn's throat as it slid down, leaving a foul, bitter taste on her tongue. "That is good."

Adele shrugged at the doctor and returned to her seat. He scowled and placed the two bottles beside Evelyn's bed, then peeled back Evelyn's eyelids to peer into her eyes. His peculiar behaviors were interrupted by a knock at the door. Frederic, The Marquess of Evermont, piled into the sickroom in a rush, quickly followed by Evelyn's ladies maid, Bess. Her brother's face was alight with joy, a countenance matched by her maid.

"Evelyn!" he cried.

"Shh!" Adele snapped. "She needs quiet, not some fool brother to yell loud enough to rouse the dead."

Frederic, chastened, tiptoed to Evelyn's bedside. He looked ragged, as if he had not been sleeping. Bess sat on the other side of Evelyn and fussed over her, wiping a cool, moist rag across her forehead.

"You can hardly blame me now for finding horses abominable," Frederic said, with a smile that looked closer to tears. "I will never ride again, and I will forbid you from doing so as well."

Evelyn made a croaking sound. Bess, the saint, offered her a glass of wine and she took an eager gulp of it, washing away the taste of the draught the doctor had given her and at last easing the scratch in her throat.

"You will not," Evelyn rasped. She sounded hoarse and dreadful to her own ears.

"She cannot be feeling too unwell, doctor," said

Frederic, looking back at the man. "If she feels up to arguing."

The doctor nodded. "No trouble with speech is a promising sign for recovery. Lady Evelyn, how is the pain? Is your vision clear?"

"Do not bombard her with questions," Adele said, cross. "If only I could have managed to bring my doctor from home. He is not such a thoughtless man."

"Excuse her, doctor," Frederic said, staring daggers at Adele. "She is just distraught over my sister's wellbeing. They are dear friends."

"The French are prone to such emotional displays," he replied. "It may be best if Miss Bouchard is sent away, to allow your sister a proper peaceful convalescence."

Frederic pretended to consider the suggestion. "Perhaps, but she is my sister's companion, and I think her presence is more comforting than disturbing. If Miss Bouchard can manage to be quiet for a time, she should be allowed to stay."

Adele scowled at him and Evelyn thought Frederic would pay for that remark later. Adele looked ready to attack, and either of the men would make a fine target. She stabbed her needle into her cross-stitching with vigor and both of the men turned away, unsettled.

"How long have I been asleep?" Evelyn asked. The draught was beginning to take effect. She could turn her head a bit now without the sharp pains, but her mind was still fogged.

"Three days now," the doctor answered.

"We were ever so worried." Bess said softly. The maid hovered by Evelyn's side.

"Some of it has been the medicine," Frederic continued. "The doctor thought your body would recover more easily if you were kept asleep, and would wake when you were up to it."

The thought of sleeping for three full days was an uneasy one. No wonder her body ached; it protested the idleness.

"But what happened?" asked Evelyn, looking from face to face. It was Adele that finally spoke.

"What do you last remember?"

Fighting through the cloud, Evelyn grasped at the one solid thing she could bring to mind. Pemberton, but she could not just blurt out the Duke's name. They had been together, hadn't they? Riding, she thought. Yes, that was it, they had been riding together.

"Riding," Evelyn said. "Yes, a hunt! I remember the hounds barking, and I remember the field full of horses."

"It was that lawn meet you were so desperate to have," Frederic said. From his tone it was clear what he thought of both Evelyn's ideas and lawn meets in general. "Pure chaos."

Adele clicked her tongue. "You had pulled out ahead, with the Duke. There was a log in the path and he cleared it, but your mare did not. She balked and you... went over her head and into a tree I believe."

Evelyn gasped as events fell into place. She could recall pieces of the day and now the sensation of flying through the air, then nothing until she woke in bed. Her chest felt heavy with anxiety, and a question she was afraid to ask.

"Is Diadem..." Evelyn's voice wavered and she tried again. "Is Diadem okay? Was she injured?"

Frederic snorted and threw up his hands. "Here you are in sick abed for three days and your first concern is for the stupid horse that put you here? Unbelievable."

"Your horse is fine, *ma amie*" Adele said. "Though she seemed quite ashamed for her actions and hung her head the whole way home."

Diadem had never been the sort of horse that enjoyed throwing her rider, as some mounts did. Evelyn could not fault the horse for throwing her. The hunt had been Diadem's first, and perhaps Evelyn had asked too much of her, too caught up in her race with the Duke for caution.

"I am relieved to hear she is well," Evelyn said.

She wanted to ask more questions about the incident, but they were all about the Duke and she did not want to reveal her feelings in front of her brother. Evelyn searched for a tactful way to ask the men to leave.

"I will tell Lord Ashwood that you are awake and speaking," said Frederic. "The poor man has been beside himself though I told him there was nothing to fret over, all would be well. And look, here you are."

Adele looked askance at Frederic. "He was the one fretting, hmm? And who has been unable to eat a bite? I do not think it was Lord Ashwood who sent the servants scurrying for cover, *mon cher*." She grinned at Frederic.

"There she goes again. One of those distinctly French outbursts." Frederic scarcely managed to get the words out with a straight face. His lips twitched at Adele's murderous look. "Doctor, will you join me for tea?"

The Duke's Wicked Wager

"I will, Lord Evermont, thank you." To Evelyn, he said, "I am staying in the house for the week, Lady Evelyn, in order to oversee your recovery. This evening I will return to give you your next draught, but if there is anything you require of me before then, just ask."

The doctor, with a wary look at Adele, followed Frederic from the room. The three women were silent until the door closed, then Bess and Adele seated themselves on opposite sides of Evelyn's bed.

"Ask, my Lady" Bess said. "I can see the questions in your eyes fighting to be heard."

Though she trusted both Bess and Adele, it was difficult for Evelyn to reveal the depths of her feelings for the Duke. They were foolish and misguided and she had tried to stamp them out, only for them to return with renewed intensity.

"Can you tell me what happened after I fell?" she asked Adele. "It is a blank spot in my mind, but I did not want to frighten Frederic by admitting it."

"I was there just a moment after it happened," Adele said, face thoughtful. "Most of the hunt did not see what had occurred, and so continued on around you, but there was a small ring of riders. The Duke of Pemberton was there; he had dismounted and left his horse forgotten. He was holding you in his arms."

Bess's inhale was sharp, scandalized. The Duke, George Pender had held her and she could not remember it. It seemed the cruelest trick of her mind.

Adele continued. "When Frederic and I rode up, Pemberton's face was a fright. He was furious, at himself or your mare, I could not tell, but he did not want to release you to Frederic. Then Lord Ashwood rode up. Of course he offered to ride back with you, but the Duke refused. He would not let anyone else near you, and in the end, his horse was more equipped to ride double."

"Oh!" Evelyn closed her eyes, picturing the scene. Had the Duke held her close, as he had in the gaming parlor, or was it only a polite kindness, protecting her from further injury by trampling?

"Without a word he climbed back up on his horse and rode back to the manor house with you in his arms. Lord Ashwood was left befuddled, but I think he has the measure of it now. Frederic is blind to it. The dullard."

"Blind to what?" Evelyn asked, in a small voice. The hole in her memory had been filled with something that did not seem real to her, as flimsy as a dream. The Duke had held her, tenderly.

Adele and Bess shared a look.

"That the Duke is sweet on you, my Lady," said Bess, in her plain way.

Evelyn opened her mouth to speak and then thought better of it.

"He is a selfish man," Adele said. "Lord Ashwood is right to not let the Duke frighten him away. Frederic thinks the Duke has just lost his mind, being no plausible reason for his behavior that he can imagine. Foolish men, the two of them."

"How deeply can he care for me if he left before I recovered?" Evelyn asked. Her draught had left in her in a hazy, detached state. Pain lingered on the other side of it and the true depths of her emotions as well. She rather liked being on this side. Everything felt a little fuzzy and soft and her headache was a little duller than it had been just a moment ago.

"He did not wish to," said Bess. She tilted her head at Adele. "I think he was persuaded to go."

Adele did not flinch from Evelyn's heated glare. "It is for the best, Evie. You know it is true, you just do not wish to admit it to yourself."

The room was quiet. "I would like to be alone now, please," said Evelyn. She closed her eyes and did not look up from the blankets.

"I will be just down the hall if you need anything at all, my Lady," Bess said. Before she departed she poured Evelyn a glass of wine and set it within reach on her bedside table. "Shall I open the windows before I go? It's a warm fall day; perhaps the last of the good weather with winter coming on."

"Yes, Please."

Bess moved around the room, throwing open the windows to let in the brisk fall air. The breeze, smelling of apples and leaves, cooled the sweat from Evelyn's skin. She longed to be outside, out of her bedroom where there was nothing to distract her from her thoughts. Adele had not moved from the bed.

"I do not think this is a good idea," Adele said, rising from the bed. She went to her chair and moved her embroidery hoop. From beneath it she pulled a letter, crumpled but unopened. "But here. From the Duke. It came yesterday by one of his footmen who would only deliver it to me; heaven knows why he trusted me with it.

Best your brother does not know you have a private correspondence with Pemberton. I think he would be incensed."

The note was unmarked. Evelyn took it, fingers shaking from weakness and anticipation. "Thank you, Adele."

"I could still throw it into the fire if you wish." Adele smiled, wider when she saw Evelyn return it.

"You have done enough, I think," said Evelyn, but there was no heat in it.

Adele hugged Evelyn, kissed her firmly on the cheek, and left. Evelyn held the note in both hands to still her shaking, partially because she was nervous, and partially due to her injury. She rested her head back against the pillows until her heartbeat slowed. Then she unfolded the message and began to read. It was short and unaffected.

Dear Lady Evelyn Evering,

I hope this letter finds you well, or at least in a state improved from the one I last saw you in. I regret the necessity of leaving Evermont while you were still abed, but I am certain you will understand the reason for it. My actions the day of the hunt and prior to it were improper and lacking the respect due my dearest friend's sister. I apologize for my behavior and assure you it will be the last of such forwardness you will have to suffer.

My prayers for your swift recovery.

Sincerely,

Pemberton.

Evelyn tore the note to shreds and flung them away from herself. Disregarding her mood, they floated to the bed and the ground with no great haste and settled around her, a reminder as irritating as their source.

13

It was a week later before Evelyn was allowed out of her bed. The doctor had told her she would be fine three days prior to that, but Adele, never trusting the man's judgement, had refused to let Evelyn out of bed. For her part, Evelyn felt recovered, if not entirely, well enough to move about the house. At times, a wave of dizziness would threaten and she would be forced to sit before she swooned, and there was a constant mild ache in her head. All of this was preferable to another minute trapped in her bedroom.

The day was idyllic. Autumn had taken over and turned the leaves to butter yellow and flame-bright red. Apples in Evermont's small orchard hung heavy on the trees like an old matron's jewels. Evelyn, Adele, Frederic, and Lord Ashwood were gathered on the lawn, playing shuttlecock. Frederic, ever lazy, performed a half-hearted swing that launched the shuttlecock a mere three feet in front of him before falling to the ground. Adele, his teammate, groaned.

"Are you even trying, Frederic?" she complained. "They are beating us soundly!"

"Evelyn is not much better than I," he argued. "She can hardly swing without falling over!"

"Oh yes, compare yourself to your sick sister. No wonder we are losing, you have no sense of pride!" Adele swatted at him with her racket. Frederic showed a surprising amount of agility and dodged out of reach.

"No. No I do not, and I am not ashamed to say." Frederic plopped down onto the grass and tossed his racket to the side. "I am content to watch you scurry about."

She stuck out her tongue in response to his lascivious grin. "Fine then, I do not need you."

To prove her point she smacked the shuttlecock into the air and sent Lord Ashwood running after it. For an old man, he was athletic and managed to return the volley back to Adele. Evelyn and Frederic watched the two more coordinated players exchange a volley of ten hits before Evelyn hopped in and bopped the shuttlecock over to Lord Ashwood.

"Nice shot, Lady Evelyn!" he exclaimed, beaming at her. It was hard to remain aloof to the man when he was nothing but kind and admiring toward her.

"Two against one is not fair at all," Adele protested. "Is this how The Marquess of Evermont treats his guests? British hospitality, I do say."

Frederic, who had reclined back onto the grass with

his hands behind his head, called out to her, "A bit of exercise is good for a woman's shape."

Adele gave the shuttlecock a vicious hit. "Does my shape need improving upon?"

Frederic's reply, a noncommittal grunt, earned him a racket to his stomach. He leapt from the ground and gave chase to Adele, who squealed and ran about in circles with her dress hitched up around her ankles. Lord Ashwood, breathing hard from his exertions, watched the antics from Evelyn's side of the net.

"Ah, to be young and in love," he said, wistful.

Evelyn, who was thinking much the same, was saved from replying by an ear-piercing squeak from Adele. Frederic had caught her at last. With his arms around her waist, he spun her in a circle until they both fell over into the grass, laughing until they cried. Would she ever have that? She looked at the man beside her. He did not seem the sort to give chase until overtaken by laughter. An image of the Duke surfaced, but she stamped it back down and with sudden boldness, took Lord Ashwood by the hand.

"Will you join me for billiards, Lord Ashwood?" she asked.

He seemed absurdly pleased with the gesture, looking down at her hand in his. "It would be my pleasure." He closed his other hand over hers and patted it gently.

Self-conscious, Evelyn dropped his hand and led the way into the house. She rubbed her fingers on the inside of her palm. There was no lingering sensation of heat or that anxious knot at the base of her spine she had gotten when... no, do not think of him. Let Lord Ashwood in.

She was trying, truly, but it was like being given a slow pony when expecting a destrier.

Adele and Frederic joined them in the gaming parlor, having recovered their senses, and they played teams until the women grew tired of the game. Evelyn and Adele retreated to the comfortable window cushion.

"You two are growing closer," Adele said, nodding at Lord Ashwood. "I am pleased to see it. Does he make you happy, Evie?"

Evelyn watched Lord Ashwood slap a companionable hand on Frederic's back. Their heads were bent in conversation she wished she could hear.

"Hmm?" Evelyn asked. "I suppose he does."

"I know you think the Duke would have made you happier, but I know otherwise. I have seen the women he has left behind, thinking they would be the ones to win him at last. They are not happy now, and that is understating the matter."

She did not want to think about his other women, nor about the man at all. "Why are you an actress, Adele?"

If the woman found the question rude, she hid it well. Adele straightened her back and glanced at the men. They were still conversing.

"It was not my intention, of course." Adele's gaze was far-away and pained. "My family was *emigré*... fleeing the revolution."

Adele was silent for so long Evelyn began to think that was all she would say.

"They did not survive long in London. I lived with an aunt and then when she passed, her estate went to a distant cousin, who had no use for a child, or should I say his wife had no use for a child-and was unaware of her growing....well, just growing. It was not my first choice, you see, to be an actress. When the cousin installed me in the theater, I'm sure he had designs, but a woman there took me in, and instructed me. She was wonderful and as I grew she thought I had perhaps some potential there."

"And you did," Evelyn said. "You are a brilliant actress; Frederic says you are the darling of London."

With some of her usual cheer restored, Adele smirked. Modesty did not suit her. "So I am. And all is well, now. I do know what others say of me but Evie, I have only loved your brother. Truly."

Evelyn reached across the chaise to hug Adele. "And you love him well. I would be best pleased to see you marry him."

"Evelyn!" Frederic interrupted. His rudeness had not been impeded by his recent soberness. "Come here!"

Curious more than obedient, Evelyn obliged.

"Lord Ashwood has beaten me." Frederic was pouting.

"Congratulations, Lord Ashwood," Evelyn said, pleased. "Do you find, as I do, that defeating my brother is a pleasure unlike any other?"

"I do indeed, Lady Evelyn."

"Bah," Frederic said. "That is not why I called you over, to tease me."

"Oh? What then?"

"Please tell her," said Frederic.

Lord Ashwood cleared his throat. "I am planning to hold a ball at my estate, in celebration of Martinmas. It would please me beyond words to have you attend, and your brother and Miss Bouchard, of course. My sister will play hostess. She has been after me for some time to host a ball."

Adele, always excited for an occasion to dress up, clapped her hands like a child. "What a splendid idea!"

"I would be delighted to attend, Lord Ashwood." Evelyn was, in fact, eager for an excuse to travel from Evermont. She felt too much had happened here of late for the place to sit comfortably with her.

"Lovely, lovely," said Lord Ashwood.

Frederic nodded in approval. It was the right decision.

"I THINK I HAVE MADE A MISTAKE." Evelyn's voice was muffled by the pillow she had buried her face in. Adele and Bess were in attendance in her bedroom, late that evening.

"You have not made a mistake," Bess said. "His servants have nothing but kind things to say of Lord Ashwood. He is a good master and a generous man. They say he treats the lowest of staff as if they were old friends and does not engage in any of the more questionable pursuits the younger gentlemen find impossible to resist."

There was no doubt who Bess meant by that.

"I thought you liked the man," said Adele, holding up one of Evelyn's dresses before her in the mirror. It trailed over the petite woman's feet, nearly five inches too long. "This is a chance for you to be seen together and make your intention known."

Evelyn peeked one eyebrow up in response. "That will never fit you. And I do like the man, I find him a most enjoyable companion."

"But you do not love him?" Bess asked.

"She does not need to love him yet." Adele held up a pair of pearl earrings to her lobes and studied the effect in the mirror. "That will come later. If they are friends now, it is enough. You cannot refuse his proposal if he asks, Evie."

Adele's words were true, but cutting. If she refused a proposal from someone like Lord Ashwood she would have little chance of ever receiving another one from any other man.

"I do not think I will ever love in the way that you love Frederic."

"Maybe so," Adele said. "But there are many kinds of love."

"A woman cannot hope for it all," said Bess. "Love, security, passion, which of these is the most important? What will you give up to manage it? Most women are lucky to find two out of three."

The questions were Evelyn's own, given voice and thrown back at her. Adele tutted, seeming to read Evelyn's thoughts in her uncanny way.

"You will not have that passion, *non*. Not with Lord Ashwood." Adele said. "Still, must I give you the specifics of the reasons I carry for not pursuing the Duke, nor allowing him to pursue you? If you knew the true measure of the man, you would not long for him so."

Curiosity warred with sense. Curiosity won. "Yes. Pray tell me." Evelyn said, simply.

Adele sighed. Bess, ever proper, excused herself. Evelyn wondered if she did not already know what Adele would say, given the way servants gossiped.

"I do not try to dissuade you because I hope you are left bereft of love, sweet Evie. Listen, then, and on your head be it." Adele settled herself on the bed beside Evelyn. "He is responsible for the death of three London women."

Evelyn blanched. She had thought of a thousand possibilities when considering Adele's warning her off of the Duke, but murder had never been one of them.

"I do not believe you."

"It is true," Adele insisted. "He did not push the knife in, but the deaths are on his conscience all the same."

"Explain yourself, Adele, or I will assume you are trying to frighten me with ghoulish tales better left to your French novels."

"Fine. One was murdered by her husband when her affair was discovered. The second was found dead in the streets; she had died from an addiction she was introduced to by the Duke. The third... " Adele's voice caught. "She was stabbed by cut throats. She was my friend"

Evelyn was horrified "Why have I never heard of this?" Coincidence was one thing, and may account for a single of those incidents, but three? "Why is Frederic friends with the man, if these stories are true?"

"They were not members of *Ton,* these women that died," said Adele, with bitterness. "And Frederic believes the Duke's side of things, that these were all accidents, some bad misfortune that follows him. Frederic cannot see that the Duke makes his own misfortune."

"And you do not agree, with Frederic?"

"I think that three women have wound up dead after falling in love with the Duke of Pemberton. He carries on, untouchable. I do not want to see you as the fourth."

"Then it is not my heart, but my very life that you fear for with the Duke?" Evelyn asked shocked.

"It is both," Adele said. "He does nothing but toy with women. They throw themselves after him, and he feigns interest or affection, and then moves on. They wallow, or die, and he does not mourn them. He is heartless, Evie. I truly believe it so."

Evelyn could not. The Duke had been callous and infuriating when she had first met him, but she had seen a change in the man. Still she recalled the cold and impersonal note he had written her. The way he had left her when she was ill…

"Will you help me choose a dress for the ball?" Evelyn asked finally. Her voice was thick with emotion but she refused to acknowledge it.

Adele smiled, relieved. "I would love to, *ma chére*. You will be a vision, and Lord Ashwood will be entranced."

14

"A box has arrived for you, Lady Evelyn," the footman said. He had a flat box wrapped in a red ribbon tucked beneath his arm.

Evelyn, alone in the entry hall, took the package from the man. He left the way he had come, down the servants' hallway, and she went up to her room before opening it. Something about the red ribbon unsettled her. The box was splattered with rain drops. Lord Ashwood had gone home to bring news of the ball to his sister, leaving Evermont quiet and eerie in the grey weather. Safe in her bedroom, Evelyn sat down on the bed with the box in front of her. She could not find a note, and the box was plain but for the ribbon. She tugged at the long end of it and the silk unraveled, falling to the sides of the box.

She lifted the lid and peeled back the protective fabric. A dress was folded inside. The fabric was fine silk dyed a deep blood red. When she pulled the dress from the box to inspect it further, a note slid out onto the floor. In familiar handwriting it said:

The dress maker will arrive at three.

Evelyn frowned down at the note. The last time she had destroyed the Duke's message it had not been so dramatic as she hoped, she threw this one into the fire. Did he expect her to accept such a gift? He was lucky it had not been Frederic who had received the box at the door. Standing in front of the mirror, she held the dress up in front of herself. It was far lovelier than anything she owned, being new and cut to the latest style. The fabric alone must have cost more than three of her dresses.

It was an inappropriate, extravagant gift and she should throw it into the fire with the note. She would have, if it would not be a crime to destroy such a dress. Evelyn hugged the gown and pressed it to herself, indulging in a moment of fancy.

"What is that?" Adele asked, standing in the doorway. Evelyn had left her bedroom door open in her eagerness to unwrap the present. "Did you go shopping without me? Little wretch!"

Feeling guilty, Evelyn tossed the dress onto her bed as if it were nothing at all to her. Adele, ever too-sharp, arched an incredulous eyebrow.

"I did not go shopping," Evelyn said. Unable to meet Adele's eyes, she folded the dress into a tidy square and laid it back in the box. She set the lid on and retied the ribbon.

"Is it from Lord Ashwood?" Adele's tone said she did not believe it was. "That was kind of him. It does not seem to be his color."

Evelyn enjoyed having a friend, but at times she wished for a less nosy one. This was one of those times.

"No, it is not from Lord Ashwood," Evelyn said.

Adele groaned in dramatic fashion. "From Pemberton, then. That fool. Your brother, oblivious until now, cannot miss the meaning of such a gift. Indeed, no one can miss the meaning of such a dress."

"Frederic did not see it, and I will not tell him," said Evelyn. "I do not intend to wear it."

"No? But it seems a shame to waste it, for it is not the dress's fault that the buyer is a bloody cur," Adele said with a grin.

"Adele!" Evelyn gasped, shocked at her language. "He is a Duke."

"Then he is a very wealthy cur, but a cur all the same."

"The dress maker will be here in a moment," Evelyn said. She could not find a response to Adele's rudeness, perhaps because she did not entirely disagree with her. "Should I send her away?"

"What harm will it cause to have it fitted?" Adele asked.

"Maybe you can take it," Evelyn said. "Yes, that is perfect. You have it."

Droll, Adele answered, "But I think it is too expensive for me."

An hour later, Evelyn was standing very still as a woman with a French accent thicker than Adele's fitted the dress. Adele sat in the corner, idle in between bouts of French with the woman. She was offering her opinion, Evelyn thought. While the other women snacked on cakes and fruit, Evelyn was forbidden from moving under threat of pin pricks and a verbal lashing in a foreign language. By the time the woman was finished she was stiff and sore.

"What did she say?" Evelyn asked Adele as the dressmaker packed up her belongings and placed the dress over her arm.

"It will be ready in three days' time," said Adele, popping a slice of apple into her mouth. "She says the Duke paid for her to work exclusively on that gown. He wanted it completed before Martinmas."

Evelyn shook out her limbs and stretched her back. A sudden faintness struck her with the movement and she sat heavily down onto a pouf. She longed for the clarity of her mind and the vigor of her body to return, so that she may ride again or even just move about the house without worrying about having a seat nearby.

"He cannot imagine I will be wearing it to Lord Ashwood's ball, can he?" Evelyn massaged her forehead with the tip of her finger. "That would be a new level of impertinence."

"Well, why should you not?" Adele shrugged. "It is not as if Lord Ashwood will know where the dress came from. Let Pemberton's behavior aid you in landing a marriage with The Marquess. It will serve him right."

It did not sit well with Evelyn. She could not decide if it was more cruel to Lord Ashwood or to the Duke. Sensing her hesitation, Adele persisted.

"It is nicer than anything you can afford, Evie," said Adele. "He wanted you to wear it, and it is certainly festive."

"I will consider it," Evelyn said. "But I thought you wanted me to have nothing to do with the Duke? Cursed as he is."

She was still hesitant to believe in any such thing. Adele did have a penchant for reading the frightening novels popular at the moment and Evelyn wondered if they had gone to her head. The man might be a rake, but that did not make him a killer.

"I doubt Lord Ashwood would have invited the Duke to Martinmas," said Adele, frowning. "They did not seem to at all get along, and who can blame them. Though Lord Ashwood is a kind and proper man, he may wish to make amends with the Duke, since Pemberton is your brother's friend and it may be awkward for them to be at odds."

If Lord Ashwood had invited the Duke, would he have accepted the invitation? The dislike had seemed mutual.

"He does not care a smidgen for propriety, does he?" Evelyn mused, more to herself. He had sent not only private correspondence but an extravagant gift. If Frederic were a more aware brother, he would have been forced to take some sort of action against Pemberton. "He acts as if we are betrothed."

"And in doing so risks making a scandal out of you," Adele said. "As I said, he does not care for the women he harms, only that he is enjoying himself."

It was harsh, but Evelyn could not refute the claim.

THE DRESSMAKER HAD BEEN accurate in her estimation,

and the dress was finished the day before Martinmas. It fit like a glove. The red accented Evelyn's coloring perfectly. She stood beside Adele as they readied themselves for the ball, and did not feel like a lesser version of beauty when compared to the actress. They both shone. Ensconced in Evelyn's rooms for the entirety of the day, the women had dressed at leisure and were at last prepared to leave the estate. Frederic, impatient, was pacing in the hall when they went down.

His face as he took in Adele was worth every ounce of delay. Evermont's coachman waited outside. The three climbed in and set off for the long ride out to Lord Ashwood's estate. They would pass by the Pemberton estate en route, but Evelyn refused to peel back the curtain and stare as if she could penetrate his walls with her gaze. She folded her hands in her lap and looked straight ahead while Frederic and Adele chatted merrily beside her.

The dress felt illicit on her skin, as warm and threatening as the Duke's touch, and it was impossible not to think of the man when she wore it. Bess thought she should have never accepted the gift. Evelyn was beginning to agree with the woman, but it was much too late for that now. The coach pulled into the row waiting to dispense passengers at the manor. Her palms were sweating in anticipation. Would the Duke be there after all? Frederic had been certain Lord Ashwood invited him, but had not heard from the Duke whether or not he would be in attendance.

The ball was hosted by Lord Ashwood's sister, Lady Lush a widow who lived at the estate with him. Adele and

The Duke's Wicked Wager

Evelyn sought her out upon arrival at the ballroom and made their introductions, while Frederic vanished into the crowd. Lady Lush looked upon Evelyn with far too much fondness. Again, she wondered what Lord Ashwood had been assured of by Frederic.

"Where did my brother disappear to?" Evelyn asked. In the crowd of faces, she could not pick out her brother's. "He has left us without an escort."

Adele stood on tiptoes to look for him. As this brought her only to Evelyn's shoulder, she had no more luck spotting Frederic than Evelyn.

"I do hope he is not looking for trouble already," said Adele.

They were saved from crossing the ballroom unescorted by the appearance of Lord Ashwood. He had spruced himself up with a smart outfit.

"Good evening," he said, bowing. "Both of you look like roses among thorns, but where is Lord Evermont?"

"I am afraid we do not know," Evelyn said, looking about again. "Perhaps he saw an old friend of his amongst the crowd."

Lord Ashwood frowned, as if he had thought of a particular friend of Frederic's. Ever a gentleman, he held a hand out to each of them. Together, they crossed the ballroom where Adele was approached at once by a gentleman requesting a dance. She accepted without hesitation.

"Shall we?" Lord Ashwood offered, gesturing toward the dance floor. The musicians, on their small stage, began a lively reel.

Evelyn smiled and slid her gloved hand into his. For

his age and his size, Lord Ashwood could dance well. He kept up with Evelyn through the reel as they wound about the other dancers, and she was the one left breathless at the end.

"Are you recovered from your fall, Lady Evelyn? You look the picture of health," said Lord Ashwood, leading her from the dance floor when the reel came to an end and a quadrille began.

"During periods of excitement I am prone to a dizzy spells," Evelyn admitted. "Although if one were to occur this evening, I would have expected it during our dance. You have a light step, my Lord!"

"Ah, I have always enjoyed dancing. It is truly the partner that makes it a pleasure."

Adele floated over a moment later, red-faced and breathless.

"What fun!" she said. "Still no sign of Frederic?"

Evelyn shook her head. Lord Ashwood, taller than the two women, interrupted.

"I do see him, and I believe he is headed this way."

"I wonder what kept him," Evelyn said. She hoped it was nothing he should not be doing, but she refused to nag on this festive day.

He greeted the trio, but appeared distracted, looking over his shoulder at the dancers and then back again.

"Now that your brother has returned, I regret I must part from your company," Lord Ashwood said. "My sister will be livid if I do not perform my duties as fellow host."

"No need to explain the wrath of sisters to me, my friend," said Frederic.

Evelyn stomped on his toe, discreetly.

"I refuse to believe the Lady Evelyn is anything but charming, as I have never seen evidence to the contrary." At this, Lord Ashwood smiled at Evelyn and said to her alone, "Though I must dance the evening with others, I will think only of you."

15

While Lord Ashwood danced with others, he was never far from Evelyn. They skirted around each other during the quadrille she danced with an earl, and partnered again for the hey. She blushed when she thought of his parting words: bold words, in front of her brother and the other dancers in the assembly room. His bald language and unabashed offering of his feelings was so unlike anything the Duke would ever do. Was it not preferable to know where you stand with a man? Why was his frankness so unnerving?

For a brief moment, as she waited for the leading lady to choose the dance, she was alone with her partner. He was a shy gentleman and had little to say, so she cast her mind about and watched the figures in the room engage with one another. Her attention was caught by a figure by the door. It was the Duke. He locked eyes with her.

"That is us up, my Lady," said Evelyn's partner, giving her arm a tug so they fell in line with the other couples.

Evelyn, distracted from the sight of the Duke, fumbled over the first steps of the dance. When she had her feet beneath her she looked up again, but the Duke had gone. She spent the entire dance searching for another glimpse of him. Her partner, understandably unimpressed by her performance, did not request a second dance for the evening, not that she would be willing to give him one. He led her back to Frederic with a sigh.

"Did you stomp on his feet the entire song?" Frederic asked, looking after the departing man with his slumped shoulders. "He was so eager to dance with you."

"Of course he was," said Adele, at Frederic's side. "Evelyn is one of the most talented dancers here. You are as graceful as a swan! I love to watch you turn about."

Frederic, never comfortable complimenting his sister, only grunted.

"I am only a bit worn out," said Evelyn. "Having not yet recovered from my fall, dancing the whole evening is proving a challenge."

"Sit, then," said Frederic. "You have danced with Lord Ashwood and that is all you need do."

"That is no fun, Frederic!" Adele protested. "Only take a respite, have a glass of negus, and you will be back on your feet again."

Had she seen him at all? She began to wonder if her mind had been playing tricks, placing a figure there she wished to see, but could not.

"Perhaps you are right," said Evelyn. "I should bow out but I do have two others on my dance card. They are both a bit later though."

The Duke's Wicked Wager

"Perhaps you will feel better after a short rest," Adele said.

The three moved to one side of the dance floor, and Frederic went after three glasses of negus. In their brief moment alone, Adele rounded on Evelyn.

"Out with it then," she said. "What caused you to dance so horribly? Was he awful and rude?"

"No, not at all. I thought I saw the Duke."

"Pemberton? Here?" Adele shrieked and turned about, as if he would be standing just behind her. "He would have some nerve to do so."

"I thought Lord Ashwood had invited him?"

"Of course, he would not snub one of Frederic's dear friends, nor a member of the Peerage. But knowing the situation, it would be the worst form of rudeness for the Duke to accept, unless he has made some private apology to Lord Ashwood, which I would be surprised to hear."

"Well, he was here," said Evelyn. "I do not know if he made his introduction to Lady Lush, but I saw him standing at the entrance to the hall, dressed to attend a ball."

Frederic returned before Adele could reply, handing a glass of negus to each of the women. The sweet, spiced wine was refreshing, but did nothing to quell the rising excitement in Evelyn's stomach.

"What has you two in such a state?" Frederic asked, indolent. "Is that a new dress, Evelyn? I cannot recall ever seeing you wear it before. It looks expensive."

"Why can you not simply tell her she looks lovely, Frederic? Why must you be crass?" Adele scolded.

The conversation had taken a dangerous turn. She

could not tell him who had sent the dress, for her would be furious at her for accepting it. If she lied and said she had bought it herself, he would wonder where she had gotten the money for it.

"I am allowed to be curious," Frederic said. "Well?"

"It was a gift," said Evelyn. A short answer was the best answer. She looked desperately to Adele.

"Dance with me, Frederic," said Adele. It was not a question, and Adele followed it up by grabbing his arm, tucking it into her elbow and near-dragging him to the dance floor and leaving Evelyn quite alone. Evelyn enjoyed a moment imagining what it would be like to be so unconcerned with propriety as the young actress.

Evelyn, now in the awkward position of being alone in the ballroom, looked about for a chair to seat herself. She should go back towards some of the other women. There were some chairs provided in the corner, and two were unoccupied, but they were somewhat secluded. Oh bother, she thought. She wanted to sit. She had only just sat down when a shadow fell across her. She did not need to look up to know who it was.

"Are you in need of an escort, Lady Evelyn?" The Duke said.

Mind racing, Evelyn tugged at her gloves, stalling for time. The kid-leather, cream gloves were as neat as they could be. She looked up.

"Good evening, Your Grace."

"May I have this dance?"

She could not in good conscience refuse him. She had the dance open on her card. She rose from her seat and he extended an arm to her. It was not improper, it was not illicit; yet placing her hand on his arm felt dangerous and made her heart race.

"That dress suits you," he said, weaving them expertly through the crowd. "I hope you did not think me too forward."

"I do think you too forward. I think you are not at all what a gentleman should be, nor did you even feign at being so."

The Duke laughed a short, harsh sound. "That is true. But then, you are not much of a lady to speak your thoughts so baldly."

"Why did you come?" she asked. "Adele thought you would not, despite being invited. She said that you had a row with Lord Ashwood before leaving Evermont. Over what?"

As they spoke, he had led them into the line of couples waiting to join the country-dance.

"I had not planned on attending," he said. "And over such foolishness as your engagement to Lord Ashwood."

She pulled her hand back. "I shall not dance with you," said Evelyn. "With everyone here watching, and knowing about the trouble at Evermont? It would be a scandal. I cannot do that to Lord Ashwood in his own home."

"One dance will not offend," he insisted.

Some of the other couples had turned to watch them argue. Face heated, Evelyn relented.

"Fine," she hissed. She did not want to make a scene. That would only make things worse.

His touch, gloved as hers was, was light and his steps were excellent. He danced without the levity of the dancers around him, and never looked away from Evelyn, even as they spun around with the other partners. She felt his eyes as surely as a touch. When they joined again, he held her closer, brushing her body with the lightest contact from his. If she had not seen his perfect steps a moment before, she might have believed it was accidental.

"You would not have accepted my gift if you felt as strongly for Lord Ashwood as you pretend to."

"My feelings for Lord Ashwood are not any concern of yours. I accepted this dance because you are my brother's friend and it would have been rude not to, not because of any affection you mistakenly believe I hold for you."

He spun away from her again and they twirled with Frederic and Adele. As the women clasped hands below, the men held hands just above.

"Pemberton, what are you doing here?" Frederic asked, breathless from dancing a double set.

"I had nothing else planned for the evening and grew bored home," said the Duke. "It seemed as fine a way to spend an evening as any other."

"You made your apologies to Lord Ashwood, then?"

"I have not."

"Truly!"

Beneath them, Adele and Evelyn had a whispered conversation of their own.

"Are you mad?" Adele asked, face pink with exertion.

"It was not my choice; he fair dragged me out here! And he is a Duke. I could hardly refuse him, when doing so would make a greater scene than accepting!"

The Duke's Wicked Wager

A new couple took the place of Frederic and Adele in the next turn. The Duke and Evelyn shared a mute, heated glare. The musicians carried on for an eternity. Each touch of his hands stilled her arguments on her lips; each absence brought them back twofold.

"It would be awkward for you to remain at odds with Lord Ashwood," Evelyn said, as he spun her around with one hand above their heads.

"I cannot see how, since you two will not marry."

"I am tired of you saying that!" she hissed.

The Duke looked over her shoulder. The song wound down at last, but they did not pull apart. He held her for just a moment in the quiet, as the other couples left the floor or prepared for the rest dance. His fingers stroked a line up her wrist.

"What should I say, then?" he asked, pitched low.

Evelyn watched his fingers dimple her gloves and longed to pull them off, to touch skin against skin. "You should just go, Your Grace, please."

"I have tried to go, Evelyn. I have tried to leave you alone, to let you marry an old man you cannot love. But I cannot. I cannot sit at home and think of you... with him."

Evelyn gasped at the fiery look in his eye. It fair burned her with a glance.

Frederic pushed in between them, an ugly look on his face. The contact and the spell between them broke, and Evelyn fled. Lord Ashwood was there, looking over the scene with a confused expression, eyebrows low and a frown on his face.

"Evelyn, wait!" Adele called. She followed Evelyn as

she left the hall, catching up with her on the front steps of Lord Ashwood's manor.

"I cannot bear a lecture now, Adele," said Evelyn. "Please, do not tell me what I should have done, or what I should not have done. Do I have no say in my life at all? Frederic, you, the Duke! The only one who does not push or pull at me is Lord Ashwood."

Evelyn leaned against the stone abutment and crossed her arms over her chest. It was frigid. She should have brought her stole. Adele sat beside her and wrapped her arms around her shoulders, pulling her close.

"I will not scold you, Evie," she said. "I only want you to be happy."

"As long as it is not with the Duke," Evelyn replied, miserable.

Adele turned Evelyn's head to face her.

Nose to nose, she said, "If you could be happy with the Duke for more than a month or two, I would give you both my blessing."

"He seems to truly care for me."

"And I am sure those women thought he cared for them, or they would not have jumped in head first, would they? I believe even he thinks he cares. I do not think he is purposely cruel, just mercurial."

The women turned, hearing voices raised behind them. A crowd was flowing toward the open doors, Pemberton and Frederic at the head. Adele and Evelyn retreated to the side as the Duke charged down the steps.

"Do not worry, Evermont," he said, half-snarl. "It will sort itself, mark me."

Frederic, a matching expression of fury on his face,

crossed his arms over his chest and watched the Duke yank his horse's reins from a groom. He drove his heels into his horse's sides, and vanished into the darkness. The crowd dispersed back inside, the women too cold to gawk if there was not going to be a scene worth watching.

"What is the meaning of this, Evelyn?" Frederic rounded on her, spotting them lurking in the shadow of the house. "What have you done to spoil things this time?"

Evelyn, outraged, opened her mouth to reply, but Adele elbowed her in the ribs.

"Not here, Frederic, do you wish to cause even more of a scene? For heaven's sake, let us go home first."

16

The women retrieved their shawls as Frederic called for the coach. It took far too long, standing in the cold, dark night for it arrive. They climbed inside in silence. Evelyn was already thinking of the letter she would need to write to Lord Ashwood, apologizing for the scene they had caused and for leaving before supper and for... well, the Duke. Though she did not think she should have to apologize for a grown man, there did not seem to be any way around it. Evelyn rubbed the silk of her dress between her fingers. It took on the temperature of the night and cooled her skin. She should never have worn it.

Frederic and Adele were silent. The coach, filled only with their breathing, felt surreal and dreamlike, as if they were traveling from nowhere, to nowhere. When it pulled to a stop outside of Evermont, Adele lightly shook Evelyn awake. She had not noticed falling asleep, but her forehead was leaned against the window of the coach and her stole had fallen onto her lap. Evelyn blinked and climbed out. A wind flipped her dress around her leg and shook dead leaves from the trees.

"Now will someone tell me what is going on?" Frederic demanded. He looked as exhausted as Evelyn felt, with purple bags beneath his eyes.

Adele led them into the sitting room and called for tea. The hot beverage, with cream and sugar, brought some life back to Evelyn.

"I do not know what there is to explain, Frederic," said Adele. "Your friend is in love with your sister."

Frederic, whatever he had suspected, was taken off guard by this. He sputtered with his first sip of his tea and set the cup down on the tray.

"Pemberton ... in love...with Evelyn, you say."

Adele gave him a withering look. "You cannot be so blind as to not have seen it before now."

Evelyn watched the conversation from a distance. Seated beside the fire, she chafed her hands together and tried to pinpoint what had gone wrong and how she could have prevented it. There was no neat checklist to avoid a scandal, however, and even less of one to avoid falling in love with a man one should not.

"Yes." Adele stirred sugar into her tea with a petite silver spoon, then jabbed it in Frederic's direction. "And he is causing quite a fuss about it. You need to stop him."

Frederic laughed. "And how do you propose I stop a Duke from doing what he pleases? He is my friend, but that only goes so far."

"He is your friend. Why do you think he should not

The Duke's Wicked Wager

marry me?" Evelyn asked. They turned to her in surprise, as if they had forgotten her in the corner.

"Well...uh," Frederic stammered.

"I have told her," said Adele.

"Oh," he said. "Well then, you know why, Evelyn. He is a fine friend, but not a suitable husband. He has no interest in settling down, and certainly not with a lady in such financial straits. Lord Ashwood is the perfect match for you, if we can manage to salvage it after this disastrous night. Pemberton has lost his head, and I will send a note off to him in the morning."

"I think that is wise," Adele said. "How are you feeling, Evie? Did the night overtax you? You are pale. Up to bed with you."

Evelyn wanted to protest, but she could hardly keep her eyes open and the pain of her head injury had returned with a dull throb, as it always did when she had overdone it. Adele tugged Evelyn's shawl tighter around her shoulders and escorted her to her bedroom, leaving her in Bess's capable hands.

THE DUKE DID NOT VISIT. Evelyn had expected after her brother's note the man would come to apologize in person, but there was neither letter nor visit from him in the following week. Lord Ashwood accepted her apology in a gracious letter, and had penned an invitation to dinner. The man was gracious and kind, to overlook her faults. Still, Evelyn could not drop the subject of Pemberton. How could the man live with himself, did his conscience not worry him to make amends for his behavior? She had needled at Frederic, pestering him to reveal what he had said to the Duke and begging leave to write to the man herself. He forbade her from doing so, of course. So she had turned to Adele.

"Would one of your servants run a note to Pemberton?" Evelyn asked, trying for a casual tone, as if she did not care one way or the other.

Adele looked up from her book, *Les Liaisons Dangereuses*. Evelyn had inquired earlier about the nature of the book, but Adele had blushed and slammed the cover closed, refusing to say a word about it.

"Absolutely not," she said. "Frederic would be livid."

"The things the Duke said the night of the ball, Adele. I would not have imagined him staying away," said Evelyn. "He seemed desperate to have me understand him. And now nothing but silence? I am worried something has happened to him."

"Nonsense. He is fine. Like as not, Frederic's letter may have knocked some sense into the man, and he has given up his foolish desire to acquire you. It is for the best. Now, it is almost three. Should you not be dressing for tea with Lord Ashwood?"

Evelyn had forgotten their engagement. Lord Ashwood had requested Frederic's permission to call upon Evelyn, in a formal beginning of their courtship. Frederic, without Evelyn's consent, had accepted. It would have infuriated her once, but Evelyn was beginning to doubt the soundness of her judgment. Perhaps something had been rattled loose in her fall from Diadem. Lord Ashwood was a good man. She was lucky he had not given her the cut.

"Yes, I suppose I should," Evelyn said. "Will you dress with me?"

"Of course, *ma chére*," Adele said, tucking her book beneath her arm.

"You can read to me from your book as I bathe," said Evelyn with sparkling eyes.

"Incorrigible brat, I will not!"

"Is it very risqué?" Evelyn whispered with a giggle.

"Stop it," Adele said. "You shan't think of such things; you should think only of how to placate Lord Ashwood. Remember you are a proper lady."

And that was just the problem, Evelyn thought. Married to Lord Ashwood she would be a proper lady, but she would never have the excitement she dreamed of with the Duke. She had to let go of this fantasy. Nothing could come of it.

Part 4

Promise Me Your Heart

17

The Lord Ashwood, unflappable man, had accepted Lady Evelyn Evering's apology with a dignified nod and a smile. She was really beginning to like the man. He was so even-tempered and kind. He insisted the issue was a minor one, and urged Evelyn not to trouble herself further over it. If only she could. She was mortified by her behavior the evening of the ball, and his dignified forgiveness exacerbated her shame.

"I was only disappointed you were forced to leave before dinner," he said.

They were seated in the breakfast parlor for a light snack and tea. Adele and Frederic, her chaperones, were seated on the far end of the room. Evelyn was certain that despite their apparent focus on a hand of cards that the two were eavesdropping to the best of their abilities.

"Yes, I am sure it was a wonderful dinner. Your musicians were excellent and the dancing never lulled.

Your sister is a formidable hostess." Evelyn poured him a cup of tea and stirred in his preferred two lumps of sugar.

"She is that." Lord Ashwood accepted the cup with tip of his head. "I do not know how she will manage being usurped from that position when I marry."

"Oh, I believe any sister would be overjoyed to see her brother marry, for the two women should be swift friends!" Evelyn said, looking over at Adele. "And there is nothing better for one's spirits than a true companion close at hand." Strange how she and Adele had undeniably become fast friends.

"Indeed," Lord Ashwood agreed. "I have friends from my schooling days who are as close as ever. Old as we have gotten, we still manage to have a raucous time when we meet, if that is not as often as I would hope."

Intrigued by the thought of a young Lord Ashwood, Evelyn hazarded a bold question.

"Lord Ashwood, why have you not married before now? The other day, you mentioned wishing to be young and in love, were you ever? In love, I mean, of course you were young. Not that you are old, no."

Evelyn's cheeks heated. When had she become a tongue-tied chit? But Lord Ashwood did not tease her, nor seem offended by her question.

"I had my share of calf-loves, yes. Even as a young buck I had far too reasonable a head on my shoulders to be carried off by amorous intent, and I think most women thought I lacked a daring sort of edge. Like the young Duke of Pemberton, now that is the sort of man I lost many a woman to: brash, indulgent, exciting."

Lord Ashwood's wry smile brought a twinge of guilt to Evelyn's heart. Here was a man aware of his flaws, accepting of them. There was something charming in that and she felt endeared toward him.

He continued, "When I was past the point of having my head turned by any pair of pretty eyes, I settled into running the estate and the responsibilities of it all. When my sister's husband passed, she took over the womanly roles in the house and we have had an easy sort of life since then, without want for anything."

"Why now, then?" she asked. "If things are settled, why change the routine by searching for a wife?"

"My sister urged me to. She is not in the best of health, being even older than I am, and worries about what will become of me when she is gone. Busybody that she is."

"You have no reasons of your own for it?"

"I confess, I had given up the idea entirely. I did not want to be married because some woman was told to, or because she needed my title or money. Now I see that there is hope for more than that, even at my age."

His look was fond and hopeful. It made her feel even more rotten for her conflicted feelings.

"I look forward to seeing your stables the next time I visit your home," said Evelyn. "If they come close to matching the beauty of the house, they will be a sight to see!"

"Are you able to ride yet? Lord Evermont seemed to think you would not want to ever again. I told him that was a bit of wishful thinking on his part."

"Already you know me better than my own brother! I am eager to ride again, and as soon as the weather turns I will be out there, whether my brother wills it or no."

Frederic, in evidence of his eavesdropping, huffed.

"I am glad to hear it. It would not seem right for you to lose such a large part of yourself. I can see you love the animals." Lord Ashwood stood and buttoned his jacket. "I must be off if I am to make it home for dinner. I thank you, Lady Evelyn, for the pleasure of your company."

"My best wishes to Lady Lush," said Evelyn, curtseying to him. "Stay dry, Lord Ashwood, and good evening!"

He dipped his head in a short bow and Frederic escorted him to the door. Adele reached up to pat Evelyn's shoulder.

"That was not such a challenge, was it?" she asked Evelyn. "I believe he is more smitten with you than ever and your affection did not seem feigned."

"It is not feigned," said Evelyn. She heard the front door open, the sudden noise of rain, then the thump of it closing again, muffling the sound.

Frederic strode back in. He clapped his hands and rubbed his palms together. "He is already inquiring as to when he might see you again! I expect a spring wedding is in the works, my darling sister."

"Why are you so eager for my marriage, Frederic?" Evelyn pursed her lips. "Do you only want me out of this house so you may redecorate, or is there something else behind all of this?"

"I am just looking out for my sister." He held his hand to his chest, pretending to take offense. "Without our parents here, it is my duty to ensure you make a match before spinsterhood. How long before you are on the shelf, a year at most?"

"I am not yet so decrepit!" Evelyn replied, but without venom.

18

*A*s if she had made it happen with wishing, the next day dawned with blue skies. Awake before the rest of the house, Evelyn dressed in her riding habit and went down for coffee.

"Whose coach is that?" Evelyn asked the servant who had brought her the tray. The nutty aroma of coffee could not distract her from the view out the window. A coach pulled by two strong horses, was heading down the long drive toward the stable.

The servant, a young kitchen boy, shifted from foot to foot. "I am not sure, M'lady."

"Are you... are you lying to me?" Evelyn asked, indignant.

With a squeak, the boy ran from the room. Evelyn, flabbergasted by his cheek, only stared after his retreating form. At least the coffee was well brewed. She finished her cup as she grabbed up her fur stole, wrapped it around her shoulders, and stepped outside. The coach had long gone, but the tracks in the mud were deep and led to the stables. Dodging puddles, Evelyn made her way down the path, grateful for the fur and the warmth of her drink. Frost edged the puddles.

It had been so long since she had gone out to the stables, she felt anxious looking up at them, as if she had lost her place there. That was silly. She belonged there. The coach, pulled by two matched greys, waited in front of the courtyard. A coachman tended to them, but she slipped by without asking after the owner. She had a hunch.

Evelyn heard Stanton in chipper conversation. Not wanting to be spotted yet, she ducked down beneath the stall walls and crept toward the men. Peeking up over the wood rail, she saw the Duke. Well, the back of him. He was leaning on the wall with one hand, the other on his hip, as Stanton gestured with a piece of tack. She did not know how the back of a man could be handsome, but Pemberton managed it. When she saw him, the affection she felt for Lord Ashwood seemed such a small, insignificant thing in the wake of her feelings for the Duke.

Stanton spotted her. She ducked her head down, but it was too late. Evelyn shook her head, frantic, but the stable master had already called her name.

"Lady Evelyn, is that you?" he asked, his arm dropping to his side.

The Duke turned. Evelyn stood and tried not to look guilty. His face tightened, a muscle twitching on his jawline.

"I thought I might visit, since I have not been to the

stables since my fall," she said, voice meek. "Is this a bad time, Stanton?"

"Not at all, I am sure the horses will be happy to see you. Diadem insists I do not feed her enough apples, but she is getting fat with laziness," said Stanton.

"Will you be riding today? Should I have her saddled, my Lady?"

The thought brought a mix of wariness and excitement to her. She felt, for the first time, a splotch of fear marring her enthusiasm for riding. It was a nasty thing which she refused to acknowledge, for doing so might make it permanent and that she could not abide.

"Yes, please," she told Stanton, before she could change her mind.

The Duke had not said a word, only stared at her as if she were an unpleasant apparition he could will away by glaring. With Stanton's departure, it seemed impossible to keep the space between them. In a rush, they both stepped forward, coming within a foot of each other.

"You did not write, nor visit," Evelyn said. "Will you always do this? Insist on being close to me, then pulling back farther than before? It is cruel."

"It is not as I planned it," The Duke said, looking down at her, eyes narrowed over his crooked nose. "Lord Evermont forbids me from entering the manor, and from contacting you. Your brother thinks I have far overstepped myself as it is, and worried that I had ruined your chances with Lord Ashwood."

"Frederic did *what!*" Evelyn fumed. How dare he leave her to fret over the Duke, while all along knowing just exactly why she had not seen hide nor hair of him. And

Adele had lied to her as well! Oh, she would have it out with them when returned to the house. "How dare he! But you have never listened to him before, have you?"

"He seemed quite serious about this." The Duke's fingers tapped on his thigh, three beats. "I did not intend to bring scandal upon you," he said softly, making her wonder exactly what had happened between them after her fall. "And truly, I thought you might agree with your brother."

"I..." Evelyn frowned. "But you are here, now."

He cocked a grin. "Well, I am not in Evermont am I? I do own these stables; he can hardly keep me from visiting them."

"How long have you been sneaking back here? Does he know?" she asked.

"Oh, a while now," said the Duke. "I come early in the mornings, when I know Lord Evermont will not be awake, but even if saw me, what would he say?"

Early in the mornings when her brother might not be awake, but he knew that Evelyn would be. She had never thought of it, how many times could she have seen him here in the morning, how many chances had they wasted?

"Will you ride with me, Your Grace?" Evelyn asked.

He was not dressed for it, but she still hoped. The Duke shook his head.

"I think your Lord brother would be furious if we were to go out riding together. No, as much as I would like to, I think it would come to blows between us if I were to dare."

From somewhere down the stable, she could hear

Stanton talking to Diadem as he tacked her up. They had only a brief moment left before the stable master would return.

"Did you apologize to Lord Ashwood?" She knew, from the way he chewed his cheek that he had not. "Your Grace."

"I am afraid that the bridge is burned too thoroughly for that. But do not fret about it; there will be no consequence for you. I can be polite if we meet at socials."

"Can you?" Evelyn doubted it.

"If he can, so can I."

"I doubt he will be the trouble," said Evelyn, under her breath.

"What was that?" He reached out and dragged his fingers along Evelyn's jawline, lifting her chin so she was forced to look him in the eyes. "Are you whispering ungrateful things after I risk life and limb to see you?"

Evelyn leaned into his touch, tilting her head toward his hand. Her retort lost its bite. "Yet, here you are, whole and hale."

"I am now." he whispered

Hoof beats on stone and Stanton's laughing remarks to a groom alerted them to his approach, gave them time to move apart and hide their guilt. Evelyn was certain she was glowing red, but Stanton, if he noticed, said nothing. Diadem was sprightly and eager to be taken out. The mare gave Evelyn an affectionate bump with her nose and snuffled at her pockets for a bit of apple.

"Silly me," Evelyn said, stroking the horse's velvet nose. "I forgot to bring an apple."

"She will forgive you." Stanton said. "Your Grace, will you ride as well?"

"No, thank you Stanton, but I must be going."

They walked together out of the stable, into the morning with its tentative sunlight. Diadem nickered to the carriage horses, who screamed replies and craned their necks to see who was calling to them.

"I will not go far," Evelyn said to Stanton. "Just a quick ride for us to get reacquainted."

"Best to not let it go too long after a fall, they say," said Stanton, with a sage nod.

Evelyn accepted the reins from his hand and tried to ignore the way her fingers shook. Her palms were sweating. The Duke was watching her. Could he see the way she fought her nerves? Embarrassed, she struggled for composure.

"Stanton," the Duke said. "I have changed my mind. Please put the side saddle on Xavier for my lady; I will ride Diadem."

The Duke took Diadem's reins from Evelyn and passed her off to a groom as Stanton hurried off to his task. "You are shaking like a leaf, Lady Evelyn. I thought I was the only one who affected you so."

"Are you jealous of a horse, Your Grace?" Evelyn teased.

"A bit."

"I thought you had decided against a ride. What will Frederic say, and all of that?"

"Frederic be damned. I can hardly let you ride alone when you are too frightened to even hold the horse. I am being a gentleman. That is the sort of thing you like, is it not? Otherwise, I shall not bother with it."

Touched by the gesture, she ignored his glib tone. Stanton was back, trotting Xavier out to them. The big chestnut's face was speckled with white.

"Here you are, Your Grace," said Stanton bringing Xavier to the mounting block.

The Duke nodded to Evelyn. "She will ride Xavier, and I will ride Diadem. He is as trustworthy as they come and will serve you well."

Evelyn stepped into the stirrup and adjusted her front leg over the pommel; settling her skirts in place. Xavier was solid and still beneath her, waiting for her cue before he moved off. Diadem danced as Pemberton mounted, but he reined her in and patted her neck until she settled.

"Shall we stick to the fields? Leave the forest for another day?" The Duke asked, taking the lead.

She nudged Xavier in to follow Diadem, and they picked their way across the courtyard and out beside the pastures. Stanton waved farewell. His expression was unreadable. Did he disapprove? Would he tell Frederic?

"Do you think I am frightened of the wood now?" Evelyn was not sure if she was or was not, but she did not want to admit it to the Duke either way.

"Maybe I am the one afraid," said the Duke, turning round in the saddle to wink at her. She scowled back. "I would like to see the orchard. We do not have apples at Pemberton."

Evelyn directed him toward the orchards and forced her hands to loosen their death-grip on the reins. A pheasant broke from the brush just before them. Diadem panicked and jumped to one side, but Pemberton held tight. Xavier, placid as promised, only raised his head in curiosity, as if he wished to see what all of the fuss was about. The Duke had Diadem settled again, though her nostrils flared and she blew a forceful breath out her nose.

"We are all right, girl, nothing to fuss about," he told the mare. She flicked her ears back, as if considering what he had to say, but danced around the area the pheasant had flown from like it might attack her again. "Are you alright, Lady Evelyn?"

Evelyn, whose heart had responded like Diadem, with panic, thumped in her ears. "Yes, thanks to this dear horse. He is a sweetheart, Your Grace. Why ever did you buy him? Xavier seems the furthest thing from your usual sort of hot-blooded stock."

"Ah, he came up for sale just last week and I thought he might be a good fit for the stable at Evermont," said the Duke.

"For Frederic?" asked Evelyn. "That is optimistic of you. Whatever the horse, I do not think he would choose to ride it."

"Mmm," said the Duke, noncommittally.

"You did not buy the horse for Frederic." Evelyn narrowed her eyes at his back. She could see it shaking with laughter and wished she had something to throw at him.

"I thought one of the Evering siblings would benefit from Xavier's sweet temper," he said.

"It will not rub off on me, if that is what you are

hoping for," Evelyn quipped back at him. "So you may as well take him back. Go on, give me my mare."

She pulled Xavier to halt, but the Duke did not slow. He lifted one hand in a careless wave.

"It is too late for that," he said, over his shoulder. "I have grown quite attached to her, rude, impertinent thing that she is. She keeps me on my toes. All she needs is to be put in her place once and a while."

They passed beyond the pastures where the horses grazed and crossed over a low stone bridge. Up ahead, the little apple orchard sprawled on a hill. Most of the apples were picked but the orchard had a sweet scent. The morning fog was burning off of it, cloaking the trunks of the trees and the few dew-polished apples. The Duke dismounted and looped Diadem's lead to a low branch, then helped Evelyn dismount from Xavier, who they left ground tied to wander through the orchard. Content to pull leaves from the apple tree Diadem paid her rider no mind as they picked their way through the orchard without the horses.

Evelyn's hem was soaked with dew in moments, but her boots kept the worst of it from her feet. The Duke walked a careful distance from her. For a time, they were content to stroll in silence around the trees. A thousand thoughts plagued Evelyn's mind, too many to speak at once. Adele's words, her dire warnings, were an ever-present mark on her feelings for the Duke. When he stopped to pluck a lone golden apple from a high branch, she managed to work up the nerve to ask him.

"What is it?" The Duke asked, catching her staring at him. He rubbed the apple dry with the sleeve of his jacket and handed it to Evelyn. He searched out a second apple in among the bare branches and pulled it for himself.

"Adele told me something about you," Evelyn began, looking at her distorted reflection in the apple's shiny skin. "Just stories. I do not believe them, truly, but…"

His face had fallen. He bounced the apple in his palm, once, twice; then closed his hand around it.

"What sort of stories?" he said. There was an edge to his voice she had not heard from him before, at least, not directed at her. It chilled her more than the breeze.

"She said you, well, that three women had died, because of you," Evelyn said, in a rush. It seemed such a foolish notion now, with the man in front of her looking, if not harmless, than at least not murderous. "I told her it must be superstitious nonsense but, she insisted. She reads those awful French horror novels, you know, I think they go to her head."

"You must believe some part of her tales, to even ask me." His eyes were a challenge.

"When both my brother and my dearest friend do not think a Duke is a suitable match for me, there must be some good reason for it." Evelyn would not be cowed by his glare. In fact, it gave her some strength and indignation to fuel her argument.

"Oh, Frederic is in on it too, then?" he said with scorn. "I thought his qualms were just the usual worries of a brother for his sister."

The Duke, in a sudden fit of pique, drew his arm back and hurled his apple across the orchard. Diadem started against her lead and Xavier trotted a short distance away, but did not run.

"That was a perfectly good apple," said Evelyn, incensed. "Will you dodge my question forever, or answer it?"

"If you demand an answer of me, very well." He crossed his arms over his chest. "I had nothing to do with the deaths of those women."

"So they just happened to perish after having... involvements... with you?" Evelyn crossed her arms as well. They eyed each other with disdain.

"Yes," said the Duke. "And I paid for their funerals, out of kindness, not any sense of obligation. Does that satisfy you?"

"Not in the slightest."

"I will not give you the details of my affairs prior to you, Lady Evelyn; they are my own business. It should be enough to know that I am not a murderer." His voice was just shy of a sneer.

"I never thought you were," she said, voice rising. "But I was less than pleased to hear of your string of sordid romances!"

He raised his voice to match hers, just short of yelling. "Then do not ask! I was not a hermit, woman; I was just a boy with more spirit than sense. It does not matter now, does it?"

"Of course it does!" Evelyn yelled back. A flock of birds squawked in protest and launched themselves from the trees.

"I am here, am I not!" His shout was more impressive. "Here with you. I have not so much as danced with another woman since the day of the match race. Does that suit you?"

Mollified, Evelyn crossed her arms. "It does!"

Pemberton snorted, sounding just like his horse had earlier. Evelyn was breathing hard as well, as if she had just run a race. He stalked toward her. She froze, like a deer upon seeing the hunter approach, believing if it stood still enough it would escape unharmed. When he reached her, just close enough to touch, he stopped.

"You are infuriating," he whispered, into her neck.

She shivered at the touch of his breath on her skin and arched closer. "If I were half as infuriating as you, I would find that an insult."

His fingers traced the skin his breath had warmed, then trailed through her hair with a tug knocking her hat askew. "Wretch." She admonished.

When he went to pull away, Evelyn grabbed his arms and held him. "Lord Ashwood will propose before winter."

The Duke's lip curled.

"Am I to say no, and die a spinster?" Evelyn dropped his wrists and spun away. "You are a selfish man."

"Your brother is never going to allow us to marry," the Duke said softly. "He has said as much to you, and made it clear with fewer words to me. What would you have me do? Do you want to be outcast from your family?"

"My brother goes to London and picks out an actress to bring home, and he states his intention to marry her!" Evelyn raged. "Why am I forced to make a match to his liking, when he might do however he pleases?"

"I do not think your brother sees it that way. He only wants you to be safe and secure," said the Duke. "With someone...not me."

The Duke's Wicked Wager

Evelyn felt as if she was standing on her toes at the edge of a precipice, danger sent all of her nerves alight. There was something hanging in this moment, a decision she could not turn back from.

"Are you afraid, Your Grace?" she said, coldly. "Is that what this is? You hem and haw about this not because of what my brother says, but because you are afraid?"

The Duke barked a laugh and she rounded on him, poking in the chest with her finger, forcing him back one step at a time.

"That is it, is it not? Coward," she spat. "Push me away, pull me in, push me away again. Those women were not murdered, they simply died of frustration!"

"Frustration," he said, a fire in his eyes. "Frustration! It would not be the gentlemanly thing to do, to steal you out from under Lord Ashwood's nose, from your brother..." the Duke began, but Evelyn cut in.

"Do not hide behind that shield, Your Grace, for your gallantry is a flimsy thing. I cannot believe I did not see it before. My own brother has more daring than you."

The Duke recoiled as if slapped. Evelyn's hands itched to do just that, half to touch him and half to express how furious she was. He closed up. She watched it happen, his face shuttered with his usual contemptuous mask and his fingers taking up their drumming beat along his thigh.

"I will escort you home, Lady Evelyn," he said. "I can see this ride has made you overwrought."

He was incorrigible. How had she not seen it before? She did not wait for him, but marched over to Diadem, caught the reins and pulled her to the nearest stump.

Hiking up her skirts, she climbed into the saddle without any aid. She yanked her skirts loose and sat astride with the warmth of the horse between her legs and her riding habit, flurried out around her. Fury had replaced fear. She dug her heels into the mare's ribs and was off before the Duke had collected Xavier who had wandered a bit farther afield. He called out to her but she ignored him, and the mare's eager stride took her away, across the orchard and into the field. There would never be anything between her and the Duke. She had no time for cowards and liars, men too weak to admit their feelings to themselves, let alone to another.

Diadem, ever a racehorse, flew across the field. Her mane whipped against Evelyn's face as she leaned over the horses neck, urging her on. Alone, Evelyn cantered into the stable courtyard. Stanton hurried out.

"Has something happened, my Lady? Where is the Duke?" he asked, reaching up to hold Diadem's head as Evelyn dismounted, yanking her skirts into place.

"He is fine," she said, curtly. "He will be here in a moment, I imagine. He fell behind. Will you see to Diadem for me?"

"Of course, Lady Evelyn," he replied. He stared from Diadem's saddle to Evelyn and back again, somewhat startled that she had ridden astride. She had not done so since long before her father's death...not since she left childhood. "Is the Duke...riding side saddle?" he murmured. His lip twitched in amusement.

There was no hope for it. It was obvious they had words out in the orchard. "I suppose he is," Evelyn shot back, thinking the grooms ride side saddle to train mounts for ladies. If the Duke couldn't stand the embarrassment, he could walk Xavier home. She didn't care.

Evelyn felt a pang of guilt, leaving the stable master standing there with a look of confusion and concern on his face. Diadem was breathing hard. Evelyn heard hoof beats growing louder and fled for the house. He could not follow her there, if he even would.

When Evelyn stormed into the house, Frederic and Adele were just sitting down to breakfast. It was nearly noon. For some improbable reason, it only added to her anger.

"Where have you been?" Frederic called, when Evelyn made to walk by the breakfast parlor. "Have you been riding?" He rose from the table and pushed the door open.

"Brilliantly spotted," Evelyn said, full of acid.

Frederic grabbed her arm and tugged her into the room so she could not escape. Adele's eyebrows had risen so far they disappeared beneath her hair.

"Alone?" he asked, with too much interest.

"Did you think I would not find out?" Evelyn asked. "That you had forbidden him from seeing me?"

Her brother smacked his hands into his forehead. "Evelyn, you did not ride out with him, unattended, this morning. Tell me you did not."

Evelyn started crying. She did not know if it was from anger or sorrow or frustration, but the tears swelled and streamed down her face.

"I will never see him again, Frederic. You do not need to scold me or warn me away, I am done with him!"

Frederic kicked the nearest chair. It skidded across the carpet and fell over in a crash near the hearth. His face was crimson. "This is unacceptable! I will have his hide, but yours first."

Adele had jumped up when Frederic kicked the chair. Unafraid, she reached out to pull him back from Evelyn.

"Calm down, Frederic," said Adele. "She is fine. No harm was done. No one knows, apart from the stable staff and who will they tell? She has said she will not do it again. Can you not see she is upset? Leave it for now. Evie, dear, go upstairs."

Adele said this all in a stream of words and punctuated each phrase with a tug until she had dragged Frederic back to the other side of the breakfast parlor and pushed him into a chair. Adele waved Evelyn away and she fled the room.

19

*D*inner was a quiet affair. Frederic refused to even so much as look at Evelyn and Adele had given up playing peacemaker. She could hardly touch her food, and Frederic pushed his around his plate more than he ate it. Adele waved away the servant's offer for dessert. When Evelyn rose to retire for the evening, Frederic looked up, bleary eyed.

"I have sent a note to Lord Ashwood," he said, voice hoarse as if he had been yelling. "He will come on the morrow for dinner. I expressed to him the urgency I feel in having you betrothed and he quite agrees with me. I expect he will propose, if not tomorrow, than shortly afterward. You will accept."

Adele must not have been told of this, for she looked at Frederic with shock on her face. Evelyn was too numb to react; she had already cried herself out this afternoon.

"Very well, Frederic." Evelyn replied softly and padded out of the room.

A short time later, a soft knock announced Adele at her bedroom door. The woman entered a book in her hands like a peace offering.

With a hesitant smile, Adele asked, "Shall I read to you, *ma chére*?"

Lord Ashwood arrived without fanfare. Evelyn delayed going down, though she had seen his coach pull up some time ago. Let Frederic have his time with the man: A chance to beg him to marry Evelyn as soon as he could. The hurried engagement would raise gossip all on its own, but he must think it preferable to the increasingly dangerous scandal brewing between the Duke and Evelyn. How much would he tell Lord Ashwood? Not much, she thought.

Adele had left her novel in Evelyn's room. The tale was a scandalous one and not at all suitable for a young woman; since her friend had only been reading to cheer and distract Evelyn, she did not take as much offense as she might have otherwise. Frederic would be furious if she stayed up here struggling through the French novel rather than heading down. He had warned her not to ruin this meeting with Lord Ashwood. Would he propose today? She imagined he would ask her to accompany him to the garden. Alone, then he would ask her. Her brother would be thrilled and her future would be secure, but is it what she wanted? Time was running out to decide.

She took slow, plodding steps down the stairs. Her father would have called it stomping and told her to act like a lady. Evelyn peeked into the room. Lord Ashwood and Frederic were at the table with half-filled wine glasses. Lord Ashwood looked excited, his round face flushed from the drink or the heat of the fire. Frederic looked nervous. She could see it in the tightness around his eyes. Evelyn stepped in.

"Lady Evelyn!" Lord Ashwood stood and bowed to her. He seemed as happy as ever to see her.

"Good afternoon, Lord Ashwood. I hope my brother has not been boring you while I was upstairs," said Evelyn, letting the man lead her to the seat beside him.

"Not at all, not at all," he replied. "You look lovely, so it was time well spent."

A servant yelled somewhere in the house and another called back. Footsteps thudded on the wood floor of the entry hall. Lord Ashwood glanced at Frederic, who raised one shoulder in a shrug but rose from his seat. He clapped Evelyn on the shoulder, and nodded to Lord Ashwood.

"I wonder what has happened." Evelyn asked. "Really, what has gotten into the servants of late?"

Frederic ignored her question.

"Lord Ashwood has asked for a private moment with you, sister," said Frederic. "And I have given my blessing."

For more than the private moment, he meant. Evelyn gulped. Was she ready? Is this what she wanted? Frederic took his leave, presumably to deal with the commotion.

Lord Ashwood held a hand out to her and she took it. His hands were warm, hers were ice. He led them out through the house and down the stone steps to the back of the house, where a small ornamental garden abutted the kitchen garden. Only a few late season flowers were in bloom. Outside, she could hear the ruckus at the entrance hall growing louder. Lord Ashwood cleared his throat. She turned her attention back to him.

"Pardon me, I just cannot imagine what all this fuss is about," she said.

"A tiff between two servants, perhaps?" he suggested. "Are you warm enough, Lady Evelyn? Should I send a servant to fetch your stole?"

"Thank you, but no. I am enjoying the bite of this weather."

"Your brother informed me you had been out for a ride – Your first since your accident, no? How did you find it?"

Either her brother had not told Lord Ashwood of the circumstances of the ride, or the man was a better actor than Adele. Nothing of discomfort or accusation showed in his tone or on his face. A shouted expletive made them both start and turn.

"Was that Frederic?" Evelyn stood on her toes as if she could see around the house to commotion at the front.

"I cannot imagine your brother using such language," said Lord Ashwood.

Evelyn burst out laughing. Lord Ashwood looked so affronted by this she nearly broke into hysterics. She covered her mouth her hand.

"I am so sorry, I am not laughing at you," she said. "It is just my brother has one of the foulest tempers. I pray you never have to experience it!"

"I would never have guessed!" Lord Ashwood

exclaimed. "He seems a mild mannered, respectable man."

Thinking of a different young gentleman, Evelyn replied, "Yes, you never can tell what is under that veneer though, can you?"

Lord Ashwood shook his head in amazement. "I suppose not."

He drew them away from the house, toward a stone bench beneath an oak tree. In its shade, Evelyn shivered. She did not want him to ask, not yet, not before she knew what to say. Lord Ashwood opened his mouth to speak but Evelyn spoke first.

"My ride was more difficult than I had expected. At first, I was frightened to mount, and then frightened when I was up there, and frightened to go at speed." Evelyn looked down at her hands. "It was an unusual feeling for me. But I hope it will subside in time. I am afraid I am just a ball of nerves."

A door slammed in the distance. Evelyn's eyes widened. Were Adele and Frederic having a row? This was their sort of thing, all drama and show. She could hear her friend's voice rising, with an actor's ability to project, over the sound of Frederic's shouts.

Lord Ashwood winced. "Well, this is not the setting I had in mind for this, but it is not that which will matter in the end, is it?"

Evelyn could not breathe. Lord Ashwood slid from the bench and knelt before her. Her pulse hammered in her ears. His mouth was moving, saying distorted words she could not understand. She blinked and shook her head.

"Sorry? Say again?"

"I asked, dear Lady Evelyn, if you would do me the honor of marrying me," he said, plainly, and with hope in his eyes.

It came to her with shocking clarity. Looking down at him, Evelyn felt many things. Affection, friendship, respect. But not love. The racket from inside grew closer. She would not embarrass him in front of whatever was happening in there.

"I am sorry, Lord Ashwood, but I cannot in good faith accept your offer," she said. "You have been nothing but kind to me, and I would be doing you disservice by marrying you."

Lord Ashwood stood with a cracking of joints and a rueful laugh. He rubbed his hand on the back of his head.

"I cannot say I am surprised," he said. "But it seemed worth a go, and your brother would not relent until I had tried."

"You knew I would say no?" She frowned.

"I may be old, but I am not blind," he sighed.

The door to the garden banged open. She could vow she heard the wood crack against the stone of Evermont. In the doorway was the Duke, looking harried. Adele and Frederic were on his heels, like birds harrying a predator from their nest. He held up a hand to silence them as his eyes met Evelyn's.

"By God, Pemberton, if you do this I will never again call you a friend," Frederic spat.

If the Duke heard him, he gave no sign of it. He

looked at Lord Ashwood, standing before Evelyn, and his eyes narrowed. Lord Ashwood held up his hands.

"Your Grace. I want no part of your temper," he said. "But you should calm yourself before approaching Lady Evelyn. She deserves none of your wrath."

The Duke's jaw clenched, but he stopped five paces before Evelyn. "Lady Evelyn, I must speak with you. Alone."

Frederic snorted. "Absolutely not."

Adele, in a small voice, said, "Maybe it is for the best if we let them alone for a moment, Frederic."

Lord Ashwood looked to Evelyn. "What does the Lady Evelyn say?"

Evelyn saw the look of determination in the Duke's face. If he did not have a chance to say his words, he may do something more foolish and dire than storming, unwelcome, into Evermont.

"Please, just let him say what he came to say" she said.

Adele grabbed Frederic's sleeve and tried to tow him back toward the house. He planted his heels, and the look he gave the Duke was wounded and betrayed. Lord Ashwood took Frederic by the other arm and together they marched him inside. Pemberton did not spare a glance for anyone but Evelyn.

"Are you pleased with yourself?" she asked him, sitting back on the bench.

"You have made yet another scene. It seems if you are good at one thing it is embarrassing yourself and me in the process!"

"What did you say?" His voice was gravel.

"I asked if you are pleased..."

"No, not to me. To Lord Ashwood. I know he was here to ask you to marry him. Well, what did you say?"

The demand rankled Evelyn. "I told him no."

The Duke looked relieved. He scrubbed his hand over his face and the scruff of hair that had begun to grow on his chin and cheeks.

"Thank God .I was worried I was too late."

"I would have told him no if you had happened to show up here or not," Evelyn said, cross. "I do not love him, and I would not marry so kind a man as he with no chance of love. He deserves better."

He sat down beside her on the bench, his body angled toward hers. "I did not come here for that, not truly."

"Did you come to fight with my brother then? For you have done well at that."

"He will forgive me. I have supported him through more mad schemes than this; he only needs to remember it."

Evelyn gripped the bench beneath her, knuckles white. "Why are you here, then?"

The Duke shifted. He stood, paced three steps, stopped in front of her, and paced three more. She was growing more anxious watching him.

"You were correct," he said at last. "In the orchard. I am a coward."

If he was waiting to be absolved, she did not grant it. She had grown tired of his flippancy, his back and forth.

"However, I was not afraid of your brother; or of Miss Bouchard, mighty as she is. Do you remember what she told you? About the women who died because of me?"

The Duke's Wicked Wager

Evelyn, unnerved by his intensity, studied the gooseflesh on her bare arms. She should have brought a stole, the stone bench beneath her sucked the heat from her body and the sun had tucked itself behind a cloud.

"Yes, but you said their demise was not your fault."

"And yet, three have died. How could I live with myself if the same fate befell you? What if I truly am cursed?" he said.

She looked at him, taking in the bags beneath his eyes and his, even more than usual, rumpled appearance. He had forgotten his overcoat and looked quite as cold as she felt, though he took less notice of it.

"You absurd man," said Evelyn. "Is that the reason you have been keeping away from me, this whole time?"

"I could not take the chance."

"Curses," said Evelyn, standing, "are not real."

"Frederic says otherwise. He was there, you know."

"Then he is a fool as well."

"I have not been thinking straight," the Duke said. He looked at the house behind him. "I did not mean to come here, only I had to tell you..."

"That you are cursed, yes."

"No," he said. "Not that."

He took Evelyn's face between his hands. He was as cold as she. His hands were like ice.

"I must tell you that I love you, Lady Evelyn."

The words were not ones she had thought she would ever hear, not from those lips. They hit her full force and left her breathless in their wake. His thumbs rubbed her cheekbones. He looked hopeful, young. For once, she did not need to question, nor think about her response. She had known it for as long as she had known the man.

"And I you, Your Grace."

In one perfect moment, they were alone and together. Consequences waited in the house, but in the garden they were untouchable. She leaned toward him, questioning. Here, he was not a coward. He captured her lips beneath his and she reached for him, hands fumbling to pull him closer. It was a clumsy thing. It was wonderful.

He pulled back. "We must do the proper thing, here, I think."

"Have you ever done a proper thing before in your life?" she asked, biting her lip.

The Duke gave her a look. "No time like the present to start, hmm?"

Evelyn would have preferred to stay outside, freezing or not. She did not look forward to what Frederic would have to say, or Adele's disappointed looks.

"Who is the coward now?" The Duke chided. He tugged her close and kissed her cheek. "I will be right beside you; you do not need to go it alone."

Evelyn nodded. They walked into the house together and were met with silence. She flagged a servant down.

"Where are Lord Evermont, Miss Bouchard, and Lord Ashwood?" she asked.

"Lord Ashwood has departed, my Lady, but The Lord Evermont and Miss Bouchard are in the parlor," said the servant.

"Three guineas that we have forced Frederic to drink again," Pemberton whispered to her. He had his hand on

Evelyn's back, a comforting gesture that kept her from going weak at the knees.

She shook her head. She would not take his bet. If she had taken the bet, she would have certainly been three guineas poorer. Frederic was staring down into a glass of whisky while Adele violently stabbed at her cross-stitching in the corner.

"Are you satisfied, Pemberton?" said Frederic, not looking up as they entered. "You have ruined it all. I thought we were friends. Nay, brothers. You have stabbed me in the back and acted as if there is naught I can do about it."

"That is not fair," the Duke said. He leaned across the desk and stole the glass from Frederic, downing the contents in a single gulp. "I have stood by you through all of your mistakes, Evermont. I dragged you from the brink in London and when everyone else abandoned you to your fate. When they questioned your love for Adele, I told them right off."

Frederic looked at Adele, then Evelyn, deciding that whatever he had to say would have to be said in front of them.

"I could support you and call you friend when the women you used up were street rats and innkeepers' daughters, Pemberton. This is different. This is my sister!"

Evelyn's face burned. She wished to be anywhere else. Adele was open-mouthed, needled poised above her work.

"I am not that man anymore. I have changed. You have changed," the Duke said, gesturing to the still mostly full bottle of whiskey. "Why can you not give me the chance to do the same?"

Her brother had never been the forgiving sort. As children, he held a grudge against Evelyn for three months when she had broken his favorite toy, and had never let her play with one of his toys again. It seemed he was still hard-hearted. Frederic grimaced and pushed the bottle away from himself, across the table.

"Do as you will, Pemberton," Frederic said coolly. "There is nothing I can say that will stop you, and Evelyn has never listened to me. I can hardly expect her to begin now."

Frederic stepped up to the Duke and wagged a finger beneath his nose; their faces inches away.

"If she comes to any harm, I will never speak to you again. I swear it," he said, and left.

20

It took Frederic weeks to move past his row with Pemberton. He walked about the house sullen as a child, until Adele told him to stop or she would leave for London and never look back. When the Duke came calling, Frederic would find somewhere else he needed to be. Evelyn worried they would never resolve it.

The breaking point came on a frigid evening during the Christmas holiday when Adele, Evelyn, and Frederic were huddled around the billiards table, nursing cups of hot chocolate and laughing at Adele's made-up rules. She always managed to win, when they played by her rules.

"His Grace, the Duke of Pemberton," a footman announced from the doorway.

Frederic shot Evelyn an accusatory glare.

"I did not invite him," Evelyn protested.

"I did." Adele pointed the billiard stick at Frederic like a sword and raised her eyebrows.

Frederic groaned as the Duke entered.

"Good Evening." Pemberton said. He was pale and pink-cheeked from the cold.

"Good Evening, Your Grace. Did you ride here?" Evelyn asked. "Why did you not take a coach? It is freezing out there!"

She beckoned him into the room and sent a servant for another cup of chocolate.

"I did not want the servants to heave to fuss," said the Duke. "And I trust a horse better than a coach, in weather like this."

"I am glad you could make it, Your Grace. I have found a means of beating the Everings at billiards at long last, would you care to learn?" Adele asked. She offered him the billiards cue, no longer needing it for a weapon.

Frederic held the other. He was looking down at his hands, avoiding the Duke's gaze.

"I doubt even that will be enough to save Pemberton from a good thrashing," said Frederic finally.

His words were met with silence. He lifted his gaze from his hands, hesitantly meeting the Duke's eyes. The playful ribbing was the first words he had spoken to the Duke since the argument the day Lord Ashwood had proposed.

"I will have you know, I have been practicing." The Duke set down his chocolate and took the cue from Adele, sidling up to the billiards table with a new confidence.

Evelyn, laughing, said, "You bought a table just to practice? Oh, you did! That is precious. Well, let us see if your hard work has paid off. Did you pay for lessons as well?"

The Duke's blush answered the question for him. "I found myself with an abundance of time. It seemed an ideal way to fill the hours."

"Now if you lose it will be all the more embarrassing," Evelyn teased.

She sat down beside Adele to watch. The fire in the hearth warmed her back, as snow piled up outside the window. Flakes fell in gusts as the storm rose in intensity, but despite its best efforts it could not penetrate Evermont and the warmth inside the manor. The Duke did lose, but he made a far better showing of it than he had in the past. Best of all, the game had been filled with the good-natured teasing she had come to expect from the two men; cautious at first, but in full swing by the last ball.

Evelyn did not realize she was staring at the Duke until he looked up at her, in the same sort of way she had been looking at him. They shared a smile. He stayed the evening in one of the guest rooms, his usual room by now, and when they woke the house had been buried in snow.

Laughing, they opened the front door and piled out into the downy snowbanks. Covered in furs, they hardly felt the cold. Piling the snow into a compact ball with her gloved hands, Evelyn began to build a horse. She had just finished the body when something collided with her back, then two more hits. Indignant, she spun around. Adele, Frederic, and the Duke were shaking with laughter, and Adele hid her hands behind her back.

"You had best not throw that!" Evelyn said.

She hardly got the words out of her mouth before her supposed friend threw the ball of slush at her. It splattered on her chest.

"Oops," said Adele.

Evelyn had a snowball in hand before the other woman could run, and she caught the French woman in the shoulder with a good hit. It devolved into chaos after that. Tentative teams were formed, with Evelyn and Pemberton against Frederic and Adele. A moment of temptation was too great to ignore, however, and while the Duke was focused on taking Frederic down, Evelyn got him in the back of the head.

They did not retreat inside until they were all sodden and shivering. Evelyn warmed herself with a long soak in A warm bath, and Adele came in as she was dressing.

"I would wear something nicer than that," Adele said, dismissing Evelyn's dress with a wave of her hand.

"Why?" Evelyn asked, suspicious.

Adele huffed. "Just do it, Evie! You will thank me later."

The Duke was waiting at the base of the stairs. Adele's words and the Duke's unrumpled appearance took on sudden meaning, and her stomach filled with butterflies. He wrapped her shoulders in a fox fur shawl of mottled grey and led her outside. A sleigh, pulled by two black horses in patent tack, waited just in front of the steps, so she could climb in without stepping into the deep snow. The Duke helped her up, then hopped in beside her and laid a fur blanket across their laps. As the coachman urged the horses forward and the Duke gave her a muff for her hands.

"Thought of everything, have you?"

The sleigh ride took them over the fields they had ridden together, and out into the woods along the cleared path between the trees. Snow billowed up on either side of the sleigh as it cut through the banks, and light flakes fell on Evelyn's upturned face. Trees looked like glass, encased in ice and snow.

"It has taken me far too long to do this," said the Duke, as the sleigh slowed and he could be heard over the sound of rushing wind. "But I hope to have eternity to make up for it."

Time stilled. Perfect silence encased them in a snow filled wonderland, and the coachman in his dark clothes faded in the background; all she could see was the Duke, turning to her with a red nose. She could not speak to reply, did not want to ruin the moment with a careless word.

"Lady Evelyn Evering, I have struggled against my affection for you. I have pushed you away. It was a fool's errand. I, George Pender, can no more deny my love for you than I might deny my own name. Marry me, and give me the joy of spending a lifetime righting all of the wrongs I have done to you."

His raw, open look was all the confirmation Evelyn had ever needed. Through tears, she nodded.

"Yes?" he asked, and she could see the brightness in his own eyes.

"Yes, you dolt, yes."

21

The day of the wedding dawned with biting cold and grey skies. Evelyn had woken early and gone to the stables with a pocket of apples. She had fed each horse a piece of the fruits. It had been a suitable distraction, but she had run out of horses and time. There was the threat of snow in the air, crisp and wet, on her walk back to the house but with all luck, it would hold off until the wedding was over.

She dressed in a silver gown, trimmed with white fur and silk while Adele, her only bridesmaid, wore pink. Frederic looked as nervous as she felt. Evelyn was thankful she had not eaten because her stomach was twisting into knots as they climbed into the sleigh to ride to the parish. Inside, Adele fussed over Evelyn's hair, straightening the silk flowers on her bonnet that had gotten knocked astray during the sleigh ride. Snow began to fall, a gentle drifting of flakes.

When the parish doors opened, her heart leapt at the sight. The Duke stood before the altar, dressed in a crisp suit; the only nod to his usual look was the gently rumpled hair that framed his angular face. Had there ever been a man more handsome? Frederic's arm was a steadying presence as they walked down the aisle, though it shook beneath hers until he handed her off at the end of the rows, to stand at the Duke's side before the vicar.

Through the lengthy reading from the Book of Prayers, Evelyn could hardly keep from reaching out to George, touching him to stay grounded in the whirlwind of emotions. The vicar passed her hand to her intended, and with clasped hands they said their vows.

"I do," said the Duke, with tears in his eyes.

"Lady Evelyn Emma Evering, wilt thou have this Man to thy wedded Husband, to live together after God's ordinance in the holy estate of Matrimony? Wilt thou obey him, and serve him, love, honor, and keep him in sickness and in health; and, forsaking all others, keep thee only unto him, so long as ye both shall live?" The vicar's voice was strong despite his age, and she felt each word as he said it.

"I do," said Evelyn, meaning it to the depths of her bones.

Adele and Frederic were crying, tears blotting the register as they gathered around to sign. Evelyn, having managed not to sob thus far, was undone when Pemberton embraced her the moment his signature was down, to whisper "my wife" into her ear. It gave her chills, to have him call her so.

All four of them squeezed together in the sleigh to ride back to the Pemberton estates.

"Do move over, Evelyn," said Frederic. "Just because you are a married woman now, does not make you any less my sister and so I may boss you around as I please."

Adele elbowed him in the ribs, judging from his grunt of pain. The Duke, with one arm draped in casual affection across Evelyn's shoulders, tugged her closer to him.

"Ah but she is my wife now, Evermont, so I may fight you over your rudeness," he said, laughing and planting a kiss on Evelyn's bonnet.

Adele protested, "She is mine, *ma chére*, and there is naught either of you may do to change that!"

"I love you all, but you must know, Diadem comes first in my heart," Evelyn teased.

They all laughed as the carriage crossed a stone bridge with wrought-iron rails to enter the Pemberton demesne. From the drive, the massive home, set behind an iced lake, stretched on farther than she could see. "Ride us past the stables," the Duke said, and although Frederic complained, the coachman complied.

"Yes, Your Grace."

Evelyn stared wide eyed at the expanse. Her own stable was indeed, a handful of horses.

"How will I ever learn all their names?" she asked, and the Duke burst into that deep laughter that rumbled into her bones.

"We will have to ride a different mount each day, My Duchess," he said with a smile. "Until every one of them pesters you for apples."

The Duke helped her from the sleigh, and the group went, with laughter and jabs, into the breakfast-scented house where the servants waited in a line to greet their new mistress. Though it was her first time at the grand estate, with George's hand wrapped around hers, it already felt like coming home.

CONTINUE READING FOR A SNEAK PEEK OF...

The Duke's Daughter ~ Lady Amelia Atherton
by Isabella Thorne

1

With a few lines of black ink scrawled on cream parchment, her life had changed forever. Lady Amelia had to say goodbye, but she could not bear to. She sat alone in the music room contemplating her future. Outside the others gathered, but here it was quiet. The room was empty apart from the piano, a lacquered ash cabinet she had received as a gift from her father on her twelfth birthday. She touched a key and the middle C echoed like the voice of a dear friend. The bench beneath her was the same one she had used when she begun learning, some ten years ago, and was as familiar to her as her father's armchair was to him.

Lighter patches on the wood floor marked where the room's other furniture had sat for years, perhaps for as long as she had been alive. New furnishings would arrive, sit in different places, make new marks, but she would not be here to see it. Amelia ran her fingers across the keys, not firmly enough to make a sound, but she heard the notes in her head regardless. When all her world was turmoil, music had been a constant comforting presence. Turmoil. Upheaval. Chaos. What was the proper word for her life now?

She breathed in a calming breath, and smoothed her dark skirt, settling it into order. She would survive; she would smile again, but first, she thought, she would play. She would lose herself in the music, this one last time.

Two Weeks Earlier

Lady Amelia looked the gentleman over. Wealthy, yes, but not enough to make up for his horrid appearance. *That* would take considerably more than mere wealth. He leered at her as though she were a pudding he would like to sample. Though it was obvious he was approaching to ask her to dance, she turned on her heel in an unmistakable gesture and pretended to be in deep conversation with her friends. Refusing the man a dance outright would be gauche, but if her aversion was apparent enough before the man ever asked, it would save them both an embarrassment. She smoothed her rich crimson gown attempting to project disinterest. It was a truly beautiful garment; silk brocade with a lush velvet bodice ornamented with gold and pearl accents.

Lady Charity, one of Amelia's friends in London, smiled, revealing overly large teeth. The expression exaggerated the flaw, but Charity had other attributes.

"That is an earl you just snubbed," said Charity, wide-

The Duke's Wicked Wager

eyed. It both galled and delighted Lady Charity the way Amelia dismissed gentlemen. Lady Amelia did not approve of the latter, she did not take joy in causing others discomfort. It was a necessity, not a sport.

"Is he still standing there looking surprised?" Amelia asked, twirling one of her golden ringlets back into place with the tip of a slender gloved finger. Looking over her shoulder to see for herself would only confuse the man into thinking she was playing coy. "I am the daughter of a duke, Charity. I need not throw myself at every earl that comes along."

"Thank goodness, or you would have no time for anything else." Charity's comment bore more than a tinge of jealousy.

Lady Amelia's debut earlier this Season had drawn the attention of numerous suitors, and the cards still arrived at her London townhouse in droves. Each time she went out, whether to a ball or to the Park, she was inundated with tireless gentlemen. If she were a less patient woman, it would have become tedious. Gracious as she was, Amelia managed to turn them all down with poise. Lady Amelia's father, the Duke of Ely, was a kind man who doted on his only daughter but paid as little mind to her suitors as Amelia herself; always saying there was plenty of time for such things. Her debut like most aspects of her upbringing was left to the professionals. *What do I pay tutors for?* He had said, when a younger Amelia had asked him a question on the French verbs. There had been many tutors. Amelia had learned the languages, the arts, the histories, music and needlepoint until she was, by Society's standards, everything a young woman should be. She glanced across the hall to that same father, and found him deep in conversation with several white haired men, no doubt some of the older lords talking politics as they were wont to do. She flashed him a quick smile and he toasted her with his glass.

Father had even indulged her by hiring a composer to teach her the piano, after she proven herself adept and eager to learn. If any of these flapping popinjays were half the man her father was…she thought with irritation.

Lady Patience, the less forward of Lady Amelia's friends, piped in, "Men are drawn to your beauty like moths to a flame." Her voice had a sad quality to it.

"I'm sure you will find the perfect beau, Patience." Amelia replied.

"Yes, well, you might at least toss them our way, when you have decided against them." Charity said. She peeked wide eyed over her slivered fan which covered her bosom with tantalizing art. Amelia's eyes were brought back to her friends and she smiled.

While Charity was blonde and buxom, Patience was diminutive, yet cursed with garish red hair. The wiry, unruly locks had the habit of escaping whatever style her maid attempted, leaving the girl looking a bit like a waif, frazzled and misplaced at an elegant ball like the one they were attending. Though her dress was a lovely celestial blue frock trimmed round the bottom with lace and a white gossamer polonaise long robe joined at the front with rows of satin beading.

Charity's flaws were more obvious, apart from her wide mouth. She had a jarring laugh, and wore necklines so low they barely contained her ample bosom. The gown she was wearing extenuated this feature with many row of white scalloped lace and a rosy pink bodice clasped just underneath. It bordered on vulgar. Amelia intended to make the polite suggestion on their next shopping trip that Lady Charity perhaps should purchase an extra yard of fabric so she might have enough for an *entire* dress.

"Do not be foolish, Patience. You deserve someone wonderful. If we must be married, it should be to someone that... excites us," Amelia said, rising up onto her toes and clasping her hands in front of her breast.

Her comment caused Patience to flush with embarrassment. It was easy to forget Patience was two years older than Amelia and a year older than Charity, for her naivety gave her a childlike demeanor.

"Not all of us are beautiful enough to hold out for someone handsome," said Patience. When she blushed, her freckles blended with the rosiness of her cheeks. Her eyes alighted with hope, and she was pretty in a shy sort of way.

Charity nodded her agreement, but Amelia frowned and clasped Patience's hands. "You are sweet and bright and caring. Any man would be lucky to have you for his wife. Do not settle because you feel you have no choice. The right man will come along. Just you wait and see."

Tears swelled in Patience's bright blue eyes. Amelia hoped she would not begin to cry; the girl was prone to hysterics and leaps of emotion. Charity was only a notch better, and if one girl began the other was certain to follow. Two crying girls was not the spectacle Amelia hoped to make at a ball. She clapped her hands together and twirled around, so her skirts fanned out around her feet.

"Come now; let us find some of those handsome men to dance with. It should not be hard for three young ladies like us." Amelia glanced back. Patience was wiping at her eyes and fidgeting with her dress— no matter how many times Amelia scolded her for it, the girl could not quit the nervous and irritating gesture—which generally wrinkled her dress with two fist sized wads on either side of her waist. Meanwhile Charity was puffing out her chest like a seabird. One more deep breath and she was sure to burst her seams.

It would be up to Amelia, then. In a matter of minutes she had snagged two gentlemen and placed one with Charity and one with Patience on the promise that she herself would dance with them afterward. Though men waited around her, looking hopefully in her direction, none dared approach until she gave them a sign of interest. She had already earned a reputation of being discerning with whom she favored, and no man wanted the stigma of having been turned away. Amelia perused the ballroom at her leisure, silently wishing for something more than doters and flatterers after her father's influence.

SAMUEL BERESFORD DID NOT WANT to be here. He found balls a tremendous waste of time, the dancing and the flirting and, thinly veiled beneath it all, the bargaining. For that was what marriage boiled down to, a bargain. It was all about striking a deal where each person involved believed they had the advantage over the other. If it were not for his brother's pleading, he would never been seen at a fancy affair like this. Dressed in his naval uniform, a blue coat with gold epaulets and trimmings and white waistcoat and breeches, he attracted more attention than he wished.

"Stop scowling, Samuel," said Percival as he returned to his brother's side from a brief sojourn with a group of lords. "You look positively dour."

"Did you find the man?" Samuel inquired.

Percival sipped his wine and shook his head. "It is no matter. Let us concentrate on the women. We should be enjoying their company and you seem intent on scaring them all off with your sour expression."

Unlike himself, Samuel's older brother Percival loved the frivolity of these occasions. As the eldest son of an earl it was very nearly an obligation of his office to enjoy them, so Samuel could not begrudge his brother doing his duty.

"You think it my expression and not our looks that are to blame?" Samuel asked, only half in jest. To appease his brother he hid his scowl behind the rim of his wine glass.

The Beresford brothers were not of disagreeable appearance, but they lacked the boyish looks so favored at the moment. They did not look gentlemanly, the brothers were too large, their features too distinctly masculine, for the women to fawn and coo over. Additionally Samuel had been sent to the Royal Naval Academy at the age of twelve, a life that had led him to be solidly built, broad across the chest and shoulders. He felt a giant amongst the gentry.

"Smile a bit brother, and let us find out." Percy elbowed Samuel in the side.

CONTINUE READING....

The Duke's Daughter ~ Lady Amelia Atherton

Want Even More Regency Romance...

Follow Isabella Thorne on BookBub
https://www.bookbub.com/profile/isabella-thorne

Sign up for my VIP Reader List!
at
https://isabellathorne.com/

Receive weekly updates from Isabella and an EXCLUSIVE FREE STORY

Like Isabella Thorne on Facebook
https://www.facebook.com/isabellathorneauthor/

Printed in Great Britain
by Amazon